KINGFISHER
An imprint of Kingfisher Publications Plc
New Penderel House, 283-288 High Holborn
London WC1V 7HZ
www.kingfisherpub.com

First published in the United Kingdom by Kingfisher 2006
2 4 6 8 10 9 7 5 3 1

A CIP catalogue record for this book
is available from the British Library.

ISBN-13: 978 0 7534 1338 8
ISBN-10: 0 7534 1338 8

Printed in India
1TR/0106/THOM/SCHOY/80NS/C

R NILY

Please return/renew this item by the last date shown.

 BATH & NORTH EAST SOMERSET

THE BALLAD OF SIR DINADAN

Bath & North East Somerset	
1 1 0479833 9	
Askews	25-May-2006
JF	£5.99

GERALD MORRIS

KINGFISHER

Love me little, love me long
Is the burden of my song.
Love that is too hot and strong
      Burneth soon to waste.
Still I would not have thee cold,
Not too backward, nor too bold;
Love that lasteth till 'tis old
      Fadeth not in haste

Love me little, love me long
Is the burden of my song.

If thou lovest me too much,
It will not prove as true as touch;
Love me little, more than such,
      For I fear the end.
I am with little well content,
And a little from thee sent
Is enough, with true intent
      To be a steadfast friend.

Love me little, love me long
Is the burden of my song.

        Anonymous Elizabethan Song
                 about 1570

CONTENTS

For Ethan, with joy.

G.M.

1

PRELUDE

"I call upon the muse of song
Or epic, like as not,
To tell a tale, but not too long,
Before it be forgot.

"I'd tell the tale of Dinadan,
A likely, quiet youth,
Whose great adventures all began,
Beneath this very roof."

"That's not a rhyme, there," Thomas said. "*Youth* and *roof*, I mean."

"It's close enough," Dinadan retorted, putting down his rebec. "I heard you use it yourself, in the tale you told last Michaelmas, about Sir Gawain and the White Hart."

"None of your lip now," Thomas said, nettled. "I never —"

"You said, 'Alas, that in the shadow of that roof, The flow'r of knighthood offered up its youth.'"

Thomas frowned. "Did I really?" Dinadan nodded, and the old minstrel grinned. "Fancy your remembering that after this long. You've a true ear for a tale. All right, so I fudged a bit on the rhyme. You can get away with that sort of thing when you're Thomas the Rhymer."

"Thomas the Humbug, more like," Dinadan said, with an affectionate smile.

"That's another thing. Your lack of respect for your elders and betters has just put me in mind of it," Thomas said, with mock severity. "Your poem's not formal enough. If you're going to sing a heroic song, you want a longer line, and you want to use your finest copperplate language, too. None of this, 'more like', or 'before it be forgot'. If you don't take your song seriously, no one will take you seriously as a singer."

"It isn't as if anyone will anyway," Dinadan said gloomily. "I'm not a minstrel. I'm a deuced nobleman's son."

"Well, don't act like it's a curse," Thomas said, half laughing. "After all, before long you'll be a knight, won't you?"

"Probably, but for what? I'll make a horrible knight, and you can't deny it. I can't do anything right!"

Thomas raised one eyebrow. "Is that what you think? Then let me tell you this. You have more skill on your instrument than I'll have if I live to be a thousand. I've never heard anyone play a rebec the way you can, lad. I just wish you'd let me teach you the lyre, too. I know it's old-fashioned now, but —"

"Why should I learn another instrument?" Dinadan said bleakly. "I'll never be a minstrel."

Thomas said sternly, "A minstrel's life is hard and hungry, Dinny. Every minstrel I know would gladly trade places with you."

Dinadan didn't smile. "Would you? Would you be me, if you could?"

Thomas shook his head slowly. "No, Dinny. Not for the world."

In truth, while many might have wished for Dinadan's circumstances – he was the son of a noted baron, Sir Meliodas of the Fens – no one who actually knew him regarded the youth with anything but pity. Not only was Dinadan a younger son and therefore less valuable than his older brother, but he hadn't even turned out to be much of a younger son. Dinadan had no aptitude for the knightly arts of tilting, swordplay, courtly dalliance with the ladies, or indeed for any of the roles of the nobility. Perhaps

Dinadan's quick wit and humour would have have made him his mother's favourite – at least, so he imagined – but she had died when Dinadan was a baby, and Sir Meliodas cared nothing for intelligence. So the baron had long ago given up on his second son and lived almost entirely for news of Dinadan's more knightly older brother, Sir Tristram.

Tristram, almost thirteen years Dinadan's senior, had left home eight years before to seek fame and fortune, and he was already being mentioned in the same breath as great knights like Sir Kai and Sir Gawain. Tristram had never returned, but the doting Sir Meliodas gleaned news of his son's heroic deeds from every traveller. Tristram had defeated a giant. Tristram had killed a villainous knight in an island fortress because the knight had insulted a lady. A few months ago had come the news that Tristram had slain a great knight named Sir Marhault.

Dinadan wasn't jealous. The youth heard the reports of Sir Tristram's exploits with almost as much eagerness and pride as his father did. Indeed, Dinadan had used Tristram's recent victory as the subject of his first full-length heroic poem. Although Dinadan's knowledge of the battle with Sir Marhault was sketchy, he had invented enough detail to make it a rousing tale, with Sir Marhault playing the role of a villainous recreant whom Sir Tristram had no choice but to slay, for the good of all England. Dinadan longed for the day when he might sing his tale to its inspiration, the glorious Sir Tristram himself.

But that dream seemed unlikely. Noblemen's sons didn't become minstrels. They might learn to play the lyre – a sophisticated instrument – and might write equally sophisticated poetry in praise of some lady or other, but that was all. They didn't learn to play the rebec or to tell heroic stories in carefully modulated tones, in speech divided into neat phrases of exactly the same length, as Dinadan had learned to do. They didn't make friends with retired troubadours, like old Thomas the Rhymer, and they certainly didn't slip away from home, as Dinadan did most afternoons, to ride carelessly through the woods, perched cross-legged in their saddles, playing and singing to themselves.

"Maybe it won't be so bad, being a knight," Thomas said. Dinadan didn't answer, so the minstrel added, "There's always the church. Sometimes younger sons become priests."

Dinadan made a face. "Is that your notion of making me feel better?"

"It isn't all that bad. You could get appointed bishop after a few years, and then you could live like anyone else – better, even. I used to play for some bishops at their feasts, and you'd never know they were holy men from the way they carried on."

"Don't think I could do that either," Dinadan said wryly. "I respect the church too little to be a priest, but I respect it too much to be a bishop."

Thomas grinned appreciatively. "Well said, Dinny. You'd be a rare minstrel, for a fact."

As it turned out, Dinadan's misgivings about his future were warranted. That very evening at dinner, as Sir Meliodas started on the third meat course and about the sixth round of claret, his eyes chanced to fall on his younger son, sitting quietly nearby, and the nobleman lurched to his feet. "What's that namby-pamby wastrel doing still here?" he demanded loudly.

The dining hall grew silent as the servants ceased their stirring and looked away. No one wanted to be the one who attracted the master's attention when he was in this humour. Dinadan waited until all was still, then said softly, "Was I going somewhere, Father?"

"Not as far as I can see!" Sir Meliodas roared. "That's the problem! How old are you now? Seventeen?"

"Eighteen, Father."

"A boy of seventeen ought to be out making his

way in the world!" Sir Meliodas declared. "When your brother was your age, he had already killed two giants!"

"It was only one, and he didn't do it until he was twenty-three," Dinadan commented.

"How many ogres have you faced, eh?"

"Only one," Dinadan replied. "I haven't killed him, though."

"There! See? You're naught but a simpering miss in boy's clothes! You should be away from here, earning glory and doing knifely... knicely... kni —... doing things. By Gor, I'd rather have you dead in glorious battle than cowering at home underfoot like this!"

"And likewise, I'm sure," Dinadan murmured.

"Here, where's my man?" Sir Meliodas demanded, looking about him with bleary eyes. His steward, Stearnes, stepped forward, and Sir Meliodas said, "Go fetch my sword, Stearnes! We're going to make a man of this milksop!"

Stearnes swallowed hard, glanced once at Dinadan, and said, "My lord, I beg you to lie down. You don't wish to hurt your son."

"Don't be such a block!" Sir Meliodas said. "I'm not going to hurt him! I'm going to knight him!"

"Knight him?" Stearnes asked.

"Knight me?" Dinadan asked.

"That's right! If you won't go out and earn the right to be knighted, then I'll knight you myself and shame you into living up to it! Hop to it, man! We'll set this boy right in the head at last, or kill him trying!"

And so it was that Dinadan was knighted. The ceremony was conducted profanely and unsteadily by the increasingly muddled Sir Meliodas, who bellowed the words of consecration and reeled drunkenly about, waving his sword with wild abandon. Dinadan stood his ground, refusing to run or to respond. At the last moment, Stearnes took his life in his hands and darted within sword range to grasp Sir Meliodas's arm before he laid the blade on Dinadan's shoulders, or else Dinadan might have begun knighthood with a missing limb or two. When the ceremony was over, Sir Meliodas managed to mumble, "Rise, Sir Dimbledum... Dumblebin... Dinderlin... oh, bugger it..." before passing out and sliding under the table. Dinadan, his cheeks bright with shame and fury, looked about the room at the shocked faces of the household. He thought of several biting comments to make about his pathetic unconscious parent, but he said none of them.

"I wish you all well," he said at last. "I'll be going now."

Two hours later, at the darkest hour of the night, Dinadan rode out the front gate of his father's home, promising himself that he would never again enter those walls. He had taken his father's second best warhorse and piled his own armour and weapons on its back, but he himself rode a gentle mare, sitting cross-legged on the saddle, fingering his rebec.

Dinadan didn't really ride cross-legged, or at least not the way a person would sit cross-legged on the ground. What he did was slip sideways, hook one knee over the horn of the saddle, and tuck his other leg underneath. He ended up swivelled about a quarter turn to his right, looking very precariously perched, but he had never fallen. He had developed this peculiar position while trying to discover a way to ride and play the rebec at the same time, and now it was second nature to him. He could ride almost at a gallop and never miss a note.

But even Dinadan could not play the rebec forever, and he had put his instrument away and was riding astride when he came upon a gaily-coloured encampment. The sun was high in the sky, and Dinadan guessed he had been riding for more than eight hours, and that without food, so he was very glad to see the circle of bright tents, each with its cook-fire in front. A few bearded men in chain mail watched him approach, and as he drew close, one stood to greet him.

Greet might be the wrong word, Dinadan thought, looking at the soldier's scowling face, but then the man's eyes fell on Dinadan's second horse, piled high with armour. "You a knight?" the man asked gruffly.

Dinadan hesitated. "I suppose I am," he said.

"Suppose?" the man repeated with a guffaw. "Are ye or ain't ye?"

"I am. My name's Sir Dinadan." The title was going to take some getting used to.

The soldier looked at the slender Dinadan with evident scorn, but he called over his shoulder, "Garth! Go tell 'er ladyship that a mighty questin' knight's 'ere lookin' for adventures." The others laughed, but one stood and made his way to the largest tent, at the centre of the encampment.

Dinadan was trying to remember what he had said that might have been interpreted as a desire for adventures, when the most beautiful woman he had ever seen stepped out of the large tent. Her golden hair fell with shimmering softness over her shoulders, and she wore a loose dress that clung to her form in all the most fascinating places. "Thank goodness!" the woman said, heaving a deep sigh and looking at Dinadan as if he were the last jam tart on a platter. "Our prayers have been answered!"

A tall man in light armour followed the lady from the tent and turned jaded eyes on Dinadan. "Are you sure, Lady Miriam?" he asked, with a slight cough. "This one seems rather young. Perhaps he is not yet ready to test himself for a lady's sake."

"Fie, Sir Annui!" Lady Miriam said. "He has a true knight's bearing! Can you not see it? I'll vow that people also doubted Sir Gawain when he was this man's age. Please, sir knight, will you join us for our luncheon? It is meagre fare, due to my sad calamity, but what we have you may share." Dinadan hesitated, glancing uncertainly at the large man behind the lady. "Do not mind old Sir Annui. In sooth, I think he envies your youth and vigour. Come, sit beside me and eat."

It was hard to tell which of those promised delights was more enticing to Dinadan. In any case, he received both. Lady Miriam sat close beside him, making sure that his plate stayed full and listening wide-eyed to Dinadan's every word. It did not seem to Dinadan that the savoury meat he was fed was "meagre fare," but perhaps they were feeding him the last good food that they had. Sir Annui, the tall knight, sat with them at first, but after a few minutes, he stood abruptly and walked away. Lady Miriam leaned close to Dinadan's ear and giggled.

"Poor Sir Annui," she said. "He's an old friend of my father's. I believe that he has some notion of marrying me, and I can never make him see that it's quite impossible. Do you not think that he's very old?"

Dinadan had not noticed this, but perhaps women had different ideas of what was too old. Lady Miriam, who looked to Dinadan to be about twenty-four or twenty-five, evidently preferred younger men, anyway. Dinadan casually stretched, then pushed his shoulders back to make them appear broader than they really were.

Lady Miriam continued. "And besides, it irks him that I've said I cannot marry until I am able to possess the land that is rightfully mine."

"What land is that?" Dinadan asked, taking another bite of roast boar.

Lady Miriam sighed and leaned her head on Dinadan's shoulder. "The land just over that hill belongs to me. It was given me by my grandfather, and just in time, too. My parents had died, leaving me penniless. I don't know what I would have been forced to do, if I had not been given the manor and the lands of Gracemoor Castle. But when I arrived to take possession, I found it occupied by a villainous knight, calling himself Sir Edmund."

"Didn't you explain that the castle was yours?" Dinadan asked.

Lady Miriam snuggled her head closer into Dinadan's shoulder. He could smell a faint perfume in her hair. "If only it were that easy," she said with a sigh. "Sir Edmund knows that he has stolen the land, but he thinks no one can stop him. He has a hundred knights, each stronger than the last. No one except Arthur himself could overcome such an army. I have no one but a few of my grandfather's servants, who are still loyal to me, and Sir Annui."

Dinadan sighed at the story of woe, but it was hard to pay attention to what Lady Miriam was saying. She was all but sitting on his lap now.

"There is one hope, though," Lady Miriam said, raising her head to look into Dinadan's eyes. "Sir Edmund is not so great a knight himself, and he is often alone. One lone knight could find him, challenge him to single combat, and slay him. Once Sir Edmund is dead, the others will go."

Dinadan imagined himself a conquering hero, earning the beautiful Lady Miriam's gratitude, but a nagging doubt intruded. "But… if that's what it would take, why doesn't Sir Annui challenge him?"

"Poor old Annui," Lady Miriam said, shaking her head. "He was wounded in his last tournament, and he cannot fight."

"He seemed fine to me," Dinadan said in

13

mild protest.

"Oh, he can walk well now," Lady Miriam said. "But he can't ride a horse. You see, the wound he received was in a most embarrassing place." She permitted herself a very small titter. "You won't tell him I told you, will you? He's very sensitive about it."

"No, no, of course not," Dinadan said, pleased to have a private joke with Lady Miriam.

"I don't know what we'll do, though," Lady Miriam said. "Just this morning we received word that Sir Edmund is mustering his knights for an attack on our camp." Lady Miriam put her arms around Dinadan and held him close. "I fear that he wishes to make me his own, and I'd rather die! Look, Dinadan!" Lady Miriam leaned away and pointed to her chest, where a jewelled dagger hung from a thin chain, almost hidden behind the low neckline of her gown. "If he should win, then I will plunge this dagger into my heart before giving in to such a tyrant!"

Dinadan tore his eyes away from the dagger and rose abruptly. "I will go to see this Sir Edmund at once!" he declared.

Lady Miriam's eyes glistened with grateful tears. "I knew you would be the one," she said, laying one hand on his arm. "But be careful, my dear. I want you to come back to me whole. You must not take any chances. Give him no chance to speak, but attack him on sight. It is what he would do to you, after all."

Dinadan nodded, his throat tight, and he managed to stumble to his horses without actually falling down. It would have been grander if he had already been in armour and could have just leaped into the saddle and ridden off, but things don't always work out as you wish. Half an hour later, mounted and clad in the armour that had never really fitted him as it was supposed to, Dinadan lifted one hand in what was supposed to be a casual, nonchalant, unworried gesture of parting, but his hand accidentally knocked his own horse's head, making the horse arch its back and forcing Dinadan to grab quickly for the reins to keep control. He tried to ride away with dignity, but he was fairly certain that he failed.

Out of sight (and smell) of the entrancing Lady Miriam, Dinadan's head cleared, and he was able to acknowledge that perhaps he had acted rashly. Lady Miriam had assured him that the evil Sir Edmund was not as a good a knight as the knights that were with him, but Dinadan had no doubt that Sir Edmund was still more competent than he was himself. It seemed likely that Dinadan's only chance of winning the battle to which he had pledged himself would be to take Lady Miriam's advice and attack on sight. It was hardly very knightly, however. If he were telling a courtly tale about a knight who had acted so, he would call that knight a rank coward.

He was still pondering his best course of action as he rode over the slight ridge of hills and came right up to two men chatting in the front yard of a small farm. One of the men was clearly the farmer, and the other was a gentleman, simply dressed but unquestionably of the aristocracy. The gentleman raised an open hand in greeting and smiled at the approaching Dinadan. "Hello, friend. Well met today!"

"Hello," Dinadan said, returning the greeting.

"Hast come far?"

"I've been riding since midnight," Dinadan admitted.

"Why, then you must come stay with me in my home. I should be glad of the company, and if you've a tale to tell, glad of that as well."

It was quite the nicest invitation Dinadan had ever received – to be greeted as an equal by a total stranger – but he replied, "I wish I could, friend. I'm looking for someone right now, though, a villain who has taken lands that are not his."

The man's brow furrowed. "Ay, I think I know who you mean. If you're looking for that crowd, then I'll surely do what I can to help you. Hang on a bit, let me finish here." Dinadan pulled up his horse and waited while the gentleman, evidently the farmer's landlord, discussed some farm business with his tenant. Then the man mounted his horse, a clean-limbed grey gelding, and rode up beside Dinadan. "We've had no trouble in this area since my grandfather's day, but it does look as if we're in for it a bit. These people came from nowhere with a motley band of mercenaries and settled in. The neighbours and I have been wondering what they were up to, and all we can figure is that they plan to take one of the local landholdings."

"I thought they had taken one estate already," Dinadan said.

The gentleman glanced at him sharply. "Not that I've heard of," he said. "Did you hear the name of the estate?"

"Gracemoor," Dinadan said.

The man's face relaxed. "Nay, Gracemoor's still safe, as you'll see for yourself in a minute. That's my home."

Dinadan swallowed. "Are you — ? What is your name?"

"I'm Sir Edmund Grace of Gracemoor."

Dinadan stared, bemused, at the pleasant face beside him. "And there," Sir Edmund said, "is Gracemoor itself."

Dinadan followed his eyes and saw a neat stone manor – too large to call a house and not large enough to call a castle – at the edge of a quiet river. "Your home?" Dinadan asked weakly.

"And my father's and his father's before him, given to my grandfather by old King Constantine himself, Arthur's grandfather."

Dinadan's mind buzzed with confusion. They rode in through the open gates of the manor, gave their horses to an elderly groom, then walked into the entrance hall. Over a huge fireplace was a painting of a grey-haired man with a glowering frown. "That's my grandfather there," Sir Edmund said. "Old Doom and Gloom, I used to call him when I was young." Sir Edmund walked through an open door into a comfortable parlour, and Dinadan took another look at the painting. Except for the difference in their expressions, the old man in the portrait bore a marked resemblance to Sir Edmund.

Dinadan followed Sir Edmund into the parlour but did not take a seat. When you were in full armour, it was sometimes hard to get out of a comfortable chair. "Tell me about these people who have moved into the neighbourhood," he asked his host.

"We don't know much," Sir Edmund replied. "They came from the northeast, armed to the teeth, and took up residence in my north meadow. I'm not using it, so I didn't object. One of them, a tall knight with a black beard and a long, pointy nose, has been down to the village asking questions – mostly asking who the largest landowner in the area is."

"And who is?" Dinadan asked. He had had no trouble recognising Sir Annui from Sir Edmund's description.

"I am. But I hardly think they'd dare to steal land from a knight, not now that King Arthur's on the throne and we have someone who will enforce the laws."

Dinadan pursed his lips. "If they did – I mean, if they were to attack here at Gracemoor – could you defend it? How many knights do you have?"

Sir Edmund laughed easily. "Knights? I don't have any knights. I told you, this has been such a peaceable county for so long, we haven't kept any at all." He glanced at Dinadan, and his laugh died. "You're not serious, are you?"

"I am," Dinadan said, with sudden resolution. It had all become clear to him. Sir Annui was trying to steal this land and had deceived Lady Miriam in the process. He probably wanted her along to give his intended theft some legitimacy. He was utterly contemptible – first to want to take Sir Edmund's land and second to use such a frail beauty as Lady Miriam for his own dark purposes. "Look here, Sir Edmund, that knight is after your land. See if you can get some of your neighbours together to meet you here, then close your gates and wait. I don't think they can have more than twenty or so men, and as you said, they're not knights, just hired infantry. But don't go anywhere alone if you can help it. He wants you dead."

Sir Edmund nodded. "And what will you do?"

"I may be able to stop the whole thing. I need to talk to someone in their camp." If he could just talk privately to Lady Miriam and tell her what was going on, she might know some way to put an end to Sir Annui's plans. Nodding decisively to Sir Edmund, Dinadan turned on his heel and went back to his horse.

As he rode back over the hill toward Lady Miriam's camp, Dinadan made his plans. He would return by a different route and approach through the woods behind the camp. Leaving his horse in the woods, he would enter the camp on foot and steal up to Lady Miriam's tent from the rear. If all went well, he would find her alone and would be able to speak to her before Sir Annui knew he had returned.

The plan almost worked. Dinadan managed to approach the camp and conceal his horse in the forest unseen. As he crept up to Lady Miriam's tent, though, he heard a murmur of voices from within. Miriam was not alone. Dinadan moved as quietly as he could in armour, until he stood right behind the tent, from which position he could clearly hear Sir Annui's voice.

"How much longer must we await your ridiculous champion?" the knight asked. "You don't really believe that stupid child could actually kill Sir Edmund, do you?" Dinadan bristled. He put one hand on his sword and considered charging Sir Annui at once.

"Probably not," came Lady Miriam's voice, and she laughed. "But what have we lost by sending him out?" Dinadan froze, his mind reeling. "If he does, by some miracle, kill Sir Edmund, then we can step in as noble avengers and kill the boy. Sir Edmund's land will be available, and no one thinks the worse of us. And, if the child is killed, all it's cost us is a day of waiting. Your problem, dear Annui, is that your mind isn't subtle enough. You just do what I say, and you'll see who's right."

Dinadan's breast felt hard and heavy. Sir Annui had not been using Lady Miriam for his own ends.

If anything, Dinadan realised, it was the other way around.

"I see one flaw in your plan," Sir Annui replied drily. "What if this child realises he's been duped by a pretty face and decides to just ride on."

"I'm not worried," Lady Miriam said. "And if you had seen his silly little besotted face, you wouldn't be either. That boy is one of those ridiculous males who'll spend his whole life falling in love, slave to every woman he meets, despised by every woman who meets him. If he can crawl, he'll come back to grovel at my feet again."

"And if he does?"

"Why then, you'll kill him, of course. I've no use for him."

Dinadan swallowed. For several seconds he wondered what he should do. He considered turning around and riding away, perhaps to join Sir Edmund in defence of Gracemoor. But he could not see how to get away without being seen, and besides, he didn't want to leave his mare and his rebec. On a sudden impulse, he walked around to the front of Lady Miriam's tent and entered. "I have returned!" he declared grandly.

"Oh, my dear!" Lady Miriam cried, her eyes glowing, "I was so worried! Have you been injured?"

"No, my lady. I am stronger now than I've

ever been."

"And what of Sir Edmund?" Sir Annui asked ironically. "Is he stronger than ever, too?"

Dinadan smiled, as an idea came to him. "It was a fight that long shall be retold," he said, lapsing almost unconsciously into the learned cadences of a troubadour. "He smote the trees, and acorns showered forth; the earth and rocks and still I stood my ground. Fleet-footed Edmund, his strength like ten men's might, drew out his sword to cleave me to the heart —"

"How did he smite the deuced trees if he hadn't drawn his sword yet, child?" Sir Annui asked.

Dinadan ignored him. "But faster e'en than he, I gripped my blade!" And then Dinadan, with a dramatic flourish, drew his sword. He meant to place the point at Sir Annui's throat, taking him off guard. After that, the plan was a bit hazier. He had a vague idea of forcing Sir Annui to admit his villainy and promise to return to whatever land he had come from. As it turned out, though, when he drew his sword, it knocked over the one lamp that illuminated the dim interior, and they were plunged into darkness. Dinadan saw a movement and heard the unmistakable sound of a sword being unsheathed. Blindly, he raised his own sword in an instinctive defensive movement.

He never completed the motion. His sword stopped sharply, caught on something, before he could get it fully raised. Panicked, Dinadan jerked on the sword, and it came free. There was no sound. As Dinadan's eyes grew gradually accustomed to the gloom, he could make out the very distinctive figure of Lady Miriam, but he saw no sign of Sir Annui. Lady Miriam stooped, picked up the fallen lamp, and blew gently on the still glowing wick. It caught, and in the growing light, Dinadan saw the knight's form at his feet. It seemed that the thing that his sword had caught on had been Sir Annui's throat. He was unquestionably dead.

Lady Miriam looked calmly at her dead co-conspirator for a moment, then lifted liquid eyes to Dinadan. "Oh, thank you, my love!" she said breathlessly. "I cannot tell you how that hateful man has tyrannised me and threatened me – with a fate worse than death! But now you've rescued me, and I am yours."

She stepped close, her hand fluttering to her breast in a very feminine motion. Dinadan saw the light flash on the blade of a tiny dagger, and he lurched backwards. Lady Miriam, her expression suddenly hard and cruel, leaped after him, but her foot caught on Sir Annui's body, and she fell face down. Dinadan backed away, out of reach of the dagger, but she didn't move. She gave a low moan, but still Dinadan stayed well clear. After a long time, reflecting that the armour on his legs ought to give him some protection, Dinadan stepped close enough to turn her over with his foot. She had fallen on her own dagger, which still protruded from her breast. Blood was already pooled on the ground where she had lain. Dinadan pulled the dagger out and threw it aside, looking curiously at the lovely face at his feet.

Her eyelids flickered, and her lips moved. Dinadan realised that she was trying to say something, and stirred by respect for her sex, or perhaps just for someone who was dying, he leaned close to catch her last words.

"Oh… bugger it," she said. Then she died.

Dinadan told the guards that Lady Miriam and Sir Annui were in counsel and, saddling his mare, left the camp. Once he was away, he took up his rebec and strummed it gently. Sir Edmund had invited him to tell a tale at Gracemoor, and now he had a good one.

2

THE NOBLE TALE OF

SIR DINADAN

Dinadan rolled over, stretched, rubbed his eyes, and sat up in the grass. The warm sun that had been so pleasant at noon, after a satisfying lunch, had grown a bit too hot and had awakened him from his nap. Dinadan drank from his water bag, then picked up the rebec, ran the bow pensively over the strings, and sang.

"Then saw the maiden how her lover fell,
With mortal wound by Dinadan's sharp sword,
And, swooning nearly, crumpled by his side.
Then Miriam prayed unto the gracious Lord

"To take her soul from her in that same breath.
Then from a chain she bared a cruel knife
Held it before her virginal, pure breast
And with a mighty plunge closed off her life…"

"No, deuce it," Dinadan muttered. "Not 'closed off.'"

It was the hardest part of his new poem, the dramatic death of the beautiful Lady Miriam, who, upon seeing her dastardly lover Sir Annui die at the hands of the noble Sir Dinadan, took her own life rather than continue without her true love. It wasn't exactly what had happened, of course, but a tragic suicide made a much more satisfying conclusion to "The Noble Tale of Sir Dinadan" than Lady Miriam's tripping over Sir Annui's corpse and falling on her own blade. Of course, it had not been easy to rewrite the facts to make Lady Miriam a tragic heroine. Dinadan could not think of Lady Miriam without shame and anger. But a tragic heroine made for a better story, so Dinadan had memorialised his enemy as a beautiful victim of love, and for his own relief and amusement had written a spiteful poem about women in general.

The "Noble Tale" had been well received when he sang it to Sir Edmund Grace and his neighbours, even though the poem was then still in very rough form. He had worked on it off and on for the two weeks he had stayed at Gracemoor, and polished the language considerably, but there were still parts that needed work.

He set aside the rebec and loaded his gear onto the horses, being careful to disguise his armour with a thick blanket. It was less complicated to be a wandering gentleman than a questing knight, who might be expected to fight someone. Since leaving Sir Edmund, he had been having a splendid time travelling incognito. He had ridden alone through the forest, singing to himself, had kept company for a while with a troupe of actors, had eaten simple meals with peasant families, and had carefully avoided every female he could.

When he finished loading, Dinadan mounted and rode off. Before long, he came upon a well-beaten road, upon which a line of carts and oxen and country people with bundles marched. Interested, Dinadan rode alongside a thickset farmer who had a basket of chickens on his shoulder. "Here now, fellow, what's to do?"

The farmer looked up at him, a bit apprehensively, but when he had looked into Dinadan's face, his own expression relaxed. "Market day in t'village."

Dinadan smiled widely. "Market day! Sounds fun! What do you do?"

The farmer now gazed at Dinadan with amazement. "'Aven't you been to a market day? I did think you was a minstrel, what with your tune-box there. You ain't a knight, are you?"

Dinadan laughed easily. "Do I look like a knight?"

"Nay. I thought you might be, at first, when I seed you with them two flash 'orses, but then I looked at you and knew you wasn't. Too friendly like. But then, ain't you a minstrel?"

Dinadan hesitated, then said, "Yes, I am, but I'm only starting out. I've never been to a market day. What should I do?"

The man seemed to accept this explanation and was happy to describe the event at length, especially after Dinadan told him to heave the basket of chickens onto his spare horse and gave him a drink from his water bag. The farmer recommended that Dinadan take a place near an alehouse and begin singing. "That's where we all go after we sell our wares," the man said confidingly. "And when we gets there, we all 'as a bit of coin. I've tossed a few coppers to minstrels myself, but only if they suit me, mind you. A bad minstrel starves even faster than a bad farmer."

Dinadan actually had plenty of money, having taken from his home everything of value that he could easily carry, but he was struck with a sudden desire to see if he was a good enough minstrel to make his own way in the world. It was a challenge, the first he had ever cared enough about to accept.

They rode into the village, which seemed not to have a name but to be called universally just "t'village," and Dinadan located the alehouse at once. It was a large building on the square where a man in bright clothing was already playing a rebec and telling a tale. Disappointed that he had been beaten to the best spot, but nevertheless intensely interested, Dinadan tied his horses to a tree at the far edge of the square and took his own rebec over to the alehouse to listen.

The minstrel was terrible. He played only three or four different notes on his instrument, and after watching him for a few minutes Dinadan felt sure that those notes were all the musician knew. The tale that was being told was one that Dinadan had heard more than once from Thomas the Rhymer, about how Sir Gawain and Sir Tor had chased a white hart and a white hound into a forest filled with dark adventures. This minstrel told the tale wretchedly, all in a gruff, tuneless, sing-song, monotone that grated on Dinadan's nerves. A portly man in a spattered butcher's apron snorted nearby. "I've heard better," he commented, to no one in particular.

"Oh, he's not so bad as all that," a woodsman beside him replied. "Remember that spindle-shanked chap who only knew two bleeding songs, and both of them little love ditties?"

"Ay," the butcher said. "That fellow could play his instrument, though. This one's hacking at it like a sawyer at a board. Don't see myself giving more than a penny for this business."

Unable to restrain himself, Dinadan said, "Don't give him a groat! He's awful! He's butchering that song worse than you'd butcher a hog!"

Unfortunately this outburst, spoken too loudly to begin with, came just as the minstrel had finished his song and was taking a bow to the silent crowd. Dinadan's voice carried well, and it was clear that most of those present heard. The minstrel flushed and looked about for the speaker. Embarrassed but defiant, Dinadan met his eyes.

"And why," the minstrel said angrily, "would you be taking bread from my mouth, child? Is it that you think you could do better?"

It had not occurred to Dinadan until that moment that his disparaging remark, intended merely as a criticism of the man's artistry, might also hurt the man's livelihood. He reddened with sudden shame. It was too easy for a nobleman with a full money pouch to be scornful. Dinadan lifted

31

his chin. "I could, friend, but I did not mean you harm." He swung his own rebec off his shoulder and gently pushed his way forward through the crowd. "I shall make you a bargain. I shall sing to this crowd, and you shall have all the money that I take in, save only enough to buy us both a pint at this alehouse. Is that fair enough?"

The crowd laughingly called its approval, and the minstrel nodded curtly, folded his arms and prepared to listen. Dinadan tested the strings on his rebec, carefully tightened one, then cleared his throat. "Today, for your entertainment, dear lords and ladies —"

The crowd laughed again, and Dinadan grinned. They were with him. He could feel their interest and attention. He looked out over the faces of the marketgoers, and he knew as if by magic exactly what they were thinking, how they were feeling, and what exactly he should do to make this wonderful, mystical connection stronger and stronger. It was the most exhilarating feeling he had ever known, and he continued almost without conscious thought: "The Noble Tale of Sir Dinadan, a great knight from the land of the fens."

"Never heard of him," called out a burly, dishevelled fellow with a red nose.

"Never heard of him?" Dinadan replied

immediately. "Impossible! And you with the look of a royal courtier, too!"

The crowd roared with delight, and even the red-nosed man grinned appreciatively. Dinadan strummed his rebec, waiting for the laughter to fade, and then began immediately on his new song. The magical sense of connection between him and his audience grew, and he began to improvise on the spot, adding new lines to almost every episode and two new stanzas describing the beauty of the doomed Lady Miriam. The marketplace grew quiet, and the crowd grew larger. Even a man on horseback passing through the square reined in to listen. When Dinadan described Sir Annui's evil plan to use Lady Miriam to steal land, there were growls of disapproval; when he sang of Sir Dinadan's mighty battle with the villain, men leaned forward intently and boys acted out battles with imaginary foes; and when he concluded with Lady Miriam's death, women (and some men) dabbed their eyes and sniffled. He finished with a long, quavering note from the rebec, then bowed his head.

The crowd roared its approval, and copper and silver coins flew toward him from every side. Dinadan grinned delightedly at the applause, drinking it in like brandy, his heart full and his head light. The minstrel whom he had replaced stepped forward, awe and respect in his eyes as he clutched Dinadan's hand. "Beg pardon, sir, for doubting you."

Dinadan grinned and waved at the coins. "Help yourself, friend."

The man did, scrabbling eagerly in the dust, and when he had collected every penny, he looked up at Dinadan and said, "I'm not forgetting our bargain, sir. I'll buy you that pint now."

The minstrel was not the only one who wanted to buy Dinadan a drink, but even better than the ale was the mutton chop and bread that the tavern owner gave him. Men gathered around him, talking in knowledgeable tones about the new hero, Sir Dinadan, and comparing him to various knights of great renown, including Sir Tristram. Dinadan enjoyed it all immensely. As he finished his meal, the alehouse grew suddenly quieter, and Dinadan looked up to see a tall young man in chain mail standing at the door. Dinadan recognised him as the man on horseback who had stopped to listen. The man saw Dinadan and strode across the room to join him.

"You tell a rare tale," the young man said. "Especially for one so young."

"Thank you," Dinadan said.

"What is your name?" the man asked.

Dinadan hesitated. It had not occurred to him

until that moment that it might be awkward to introduce himself as Sir Dinadan. He chose at random the name of his father's steward. "My name is Stearnes."

The young man sat down at Dinadan's table. "How comes it that one so gifted as you is not at a king's court?"

"Perhaps I will be one day," Dinadan said evasively.

"Well said, fellow!" the young man cried with delight, as if Dinadan had said something clever. "Why don't you ride with me, good Stearnes? For I go there!"

"Go where?"

"To Arthur's court at Camelot, of course, to be made a knight. My name is Culloch and I'm from a good Welsh family. You really ought to come to Camelot, you know. It's where all the greatest knights are, and any one of them would love to have a minstrel like you."

Dinadan had thought about going to see the great court that King Arthur had established at Camelot, but aware of his own knightly shortcomings, he had not felt that he was quite ready for such company. Now he was presented with the opportunity to see all the sights of Camelot incognito, a wandering minstrel in the company of this brash young knight. Dinadan made his decision quickly. "Very well,

Culloch. Let's go."

Culloch smiled with pleasure, but did not move. "It is a long journey, good Stearnes. I must fortify myself." Culloch signalled to the tavern keeper, and Dinadan watched with growing awe as Culloch devoured a whole leg of lamb, an entire chicken, two loaves of bread, and a heavy pudding. If he could fight as well as he ate, he would have no trouble achieving knighthood.

The trip to Camelot was uneventful, though marked with a great deal of idle chatter, none of which came from Dinadan. Culloch was bluff, good-humoured, and unceasingly communicative. He talked in great detail about knightly deeds, seldom requiring any response but a polite "Oh?" or "You don't say!" Culloch enjoyed a joke and laughed as loudly when he told it for the tenth time as he had when he had told it first. He felt compelled to show everything in his knightly wardrobe to Dinadan and to explain what every bit of armour was, but to Dinadan's relief, never showed the slightest curiosity about the large blanket-wrapped bundle that was Dinadan's own armour. Culloch ate well, sang poorly but loudly, and drank as much as he could find. All of these Dinadan treated with amusement, or at least tolerance. The only thing that bothered Dinadan about his companion was his tendency, when Dinadan was performing "The Tale of Sir Dinadan" in the various alehouses where they stopped, to call out "This is a good part!" at key moments or to interrupt with such comments as "You did it different last time!"

The two companions took their time but eventually arrived at Camelot. There, they were welcomed by the guards, who evidently had instructions to permit all wandering knights to enter, and they were shown to cramped but serviceable quarters where they could wait until the young king was able to see them. Dinadan hoped to encounter Sir Gawain, who all agreed was King Arthur's greatest knight, but Sir Gawain was away on a quest. Dinadan would have to be content with seeing the great Sir Kai, King Arthur's foster brother, who was also the king's seneschal.

On their very first night in the castle, Culloch and Dinadan were in their room, discussing the court, when there was a knock at the door. They opened the door to see a tall man with a neat brown beard and a brilliant chain around his neck. "Excuse my interruption," the man said politely, "but are you the two knights who arrived this morning?"

Culloch answered immediately. "We did get here this morning, but it's only one knight. Me.

But I'm not actually a knight yet."

The man looked surprised. "Only one knight?"

"That's right. This is my minstrel, Stearnes."

Dinadan glanced sharply at Culloch. Nothing had ever been said about Dinadan being *his* minstrel. The tall man looked curiously at Dinadan, then back at Culloch. "Then whose horse is the big sorrel?" he asked.

"That's mine," Dinadan said calmly. He met the man's eyes, which crinkled at the edges in what could have been either suspicion or amusement. If this man knew what colour Dinadan's horse was, then he probably knew about the armour that was in that horse's pack.

"I beg your pardon, both," the man said, bowing. "I am Sir Bedivere, and I've come to ask you to accompany me. The king is holding court this evening, and he wishes to hear your business." Culloch leaped to his feet, but Dinadan hesitated. "Both of you are invited," Sir Bedivere said with a smile.

Dinadan had long wanted to see the great King Arthur who, according to the tales, had risen to power by the magic of Merlin but who had managed to unite the splintered and warring land of England by some magic of his own. At first Dinadan was vaguely disappointed by the ordinary figure of the king – slender beside the mountainous forms of some of his knights, plain beside the gaily coloured figures of his courtiers – but as he watched the king conduct business, his regard grew. The king was gentle but never soft, compassionate but never yielding, quiet but always clear. He dealt first with mundane matters, such as disputes between landlords and tenants, but at last the king leaned back on his throne and said with a sigh of relief, "Now, Bedivere, did you not say we had some here requesting knighthood and fellowship at our Round Table?"

Culloch leaped to his feet and said, "Here, Sire!"

It was a breach of courtly etiquette, as even Dinadan knew, but the king only smiled and waved him forward. "What is your name, my friend?"

"I am Culloch of Wales, Your Highness, son of Sir Gwynet of the Crags."

"And you ask that I knight you?"

"Yes, Sire. It is my dearest wish to be a knight of your Round Table and to take my place with the greatest knights of all. I want to go on quest for your court, to prove myself against your enemies."

The king nodded graciously and said, "It is good to have great plans. What have you done already?"

"Sire?"

"It is the custom of this court to grant knighthood only to those who have already proven

39

themselves worthy. Have you helped the helpless? Rescued any in need? Righted any wrong?"

Culloch's mouth opened slightly with amazement. "Not... not yet. I thought I should be made knight first... my father said..." His voice trailed off.

"Your father may be forgiven for not knowing the customs of this court," Arthur said gently. "It is a new idea, earning knighthood by deed instead of by parentage. I cannot knight you now, but be assured that once you have set about your career and proven yourself in knightly deeds, I shall be happy to receive you and hear your request again."

Culloch looked so downcast as he made his way back to his seat, that Dinadan could not help feeling sorry for him. Sir Bedivere must have felt the same, for he stood and said, "Sire?"

Arthur glanced at the knight. "Yes, Bedivere?"

"This youth seems a likely lad. I have no doubt that he will do great deeds, if only he is directed well."

Arthur grinned. "Don't tell me. You'd like permission to go with him and guide him."

Sir Bedivere smiled back. A huge man with a black beard, who had stood beside the king throughout the evening, rolled his eyes and groaned. "Don't be an ass, Bedivere," the man said. "How many times do I have to tell you that you can't take in every stray puppy that —"

"But what if the stray turns into a fine hound, Kai?" Bedivere asked, grinning.

Dinadan looked at the large man more closely. So this was Sir Kai, Arthur's foster brother and one of the heroes of Arthur's wars. "And what if he doesn't?" Sir Kai retorted.

Sir Bedivere's smile only grew, and he turned to Culloch. "What do you say, Culloch? Would you like some company on your quest?"

Culloch's expression cleared. "You'll come with me until I earn knighthood? Really?"

"I vow it," Sir Bedivere said solemnly. "Until you gain it or stop seeking it."

"Oh, ye gods!" Sir Kai said with a moan. "Why did you have to vow it? I'faith, I know not which is softer, your heart or your head. I can just see you spending your life hunting dragons for someone else to slay."

"I can think of worse ways to live," Sir Bedivere replied quietly. "Surely the greatest fool is the one who only seeks his own glory."

Sir Kai snorted. "We'll see." Sir Kai turned abruptly to the king. "Arthur, I ask your leave to accompany my idiot cousin."

Sir Bedivere's eyes lit with delight, and Dinadan realised that these two knights were, in fact, the closest of friends. "And would you deprive me of two of my greatest knights at once?" Arthur asked. Sir Bedivere smiled, and Sir Kai shrugged. "Ah, well, if I am deprived, I am deprived. You may both go."

"Hooray!" crowed Culloch. "I'm going questing with Sir Kai and Sir Bedivere!"

Arthur shook his head slowly, still half smiling. "And I hope they both know what they're doing. Now, before you leave me to become knightly mentors, is there no other business? Bedivere, I thought you said there were two knights."

Sir Bedivere turned his eyes toward Dinadan. "I may have been mistaken, but I don't think so. Would you come here please, friend?" Swallowing, Dinadan rose and took a position beside Sir Bedivere. "I am told that this youth is a minstrel, but I would like to hear it from his own lips. Sir, are you a minstrel? Or a knight?"

Dinadan could not lie. "I... I am a knight, Your Highness."

"Already made knight?" the king asked. "Or one who seeks knighthood."

Dinadan flushed slightly at the memory of his knighting, but he said evenly, "I was knighted by my father." He stole a quick glance at Culloch, who was gazing at him with open-mouthed amazement.

"And what is your name, friend?" asked the king.

"It's Dina — I mean, *Sir* Dinadan."

There was a mild commotion in the throne room as knights and ladies and courtiers whispered to each other excitedly. King Arthur lifted one eyebrow. "Sir Dinadan who killed Sir Annui?"

Dinadan blinked. "Well, yes, but how did you hear about that?"

"The tale was sung to us by a wandering minstrel at our dinner just yesternight. A great victory, indeed."

Dinadan was torn between pleasure that his own song was already being sung by other minstrels and embarrassment that his own embellishments of the truth must have also been repeated. He cleared his throat. "I've... I've heard the song myself, Sire, and the truth of the matter is not quite so impressive as the story."

"It never is," the king replied with a smile. "But are the essentials true? Was this Sir Annui seeking to steal lands from one Sir Edmund?" Dinadan nodded. "And did you discover the plot and face him?" Nod. "And did he draw a sword on you and you slay him?"

"I was lucky, Sire."

"It is often so," Arthur said, laughing softly but with an expression of approval in his eyes.

"Finally, did the Lady Miriam kill herself?"

"Well, yes, but it wasn't quite as dramatic as I made it – as the song makes it sound."

"What is a tale for but to make the facts better?" asked the king. "You have saved a good man from oppression, faced his oppressor, a knight older than yourself, and slain him. Furthermore, you conduct yourself with commendable humility – and honesty. You have done a deed worthy of a fellow of the Round Table. Sir Dinadan, do you wish to join my fellowship?"

Dinadan met the king's eyes, and although he knew he did not deserve the honour he was offered, he could not refuse. "Yes, Sire. I wish to serve you in whatever way I can."

"Then kneel, Sir Dinadan." The king drew his splendid sword, Excalibur, and lightly touched Dinadan's shoulder. "Rise, Sir Dinadan, and welcome to the Fellowship of the Round Table. Be ever true to your God; protect always your neighbour; honour always your king."

3

TWO TALES OF

SIR MARHAULT

They rode away together the next morning, the four of them. Culloch went to earn knighthood, Sir Bedivere went to help him, Sir Kai went to help Sir Bedivere, and Dinadan went along for the ride. For two hours after leaving Camelot, Culloch could talk of nothing but of how Dinadan had concealed his knighthood. To Dinadan's relief, Culloch was not offended but took the whole thing as a colossal joke. Nevertheless, by the time Culloch had laughed at the masquerade for the hundredth time, Dinadan could almost wish Culloch had gotten angry. Then at least he might have been quiet, like the other two knights.

Dinadan stole a glance at Sir Bedivere and Sir Kai, riding beside him. After the throne room council the night before, Dinadan had asked a few discreet questions and discovered that Sir Bedivere was nothing less than the king's first cousin. He had been Arthur's childhood friend and the king's first knight after Sir Kai. He had distinguished himself in Arthur's wars and was one of the king's most trusted advisors. As for Sir Kai, everyone knew about Arthur's foster brother – of his fierce pride, his fierceness in battle, and his fierce loyalty to Arthur. Dinadan grinned to himself. *Fierce* seemed to be the word to describe Sir Kai.

It was certainly fitting at the moment. Culloch had just burst out with another inane laugh and said, "Hey, Stearnes! I mean Dinadan – ho ho, that'll take some getting used to, won't it? – I was just thinking!"

"Were you?" Dinadan asked.

"Yes. Yes, I was. Now, what was I thinking? Oh, yes, do you remember that minstrel you outsang at the market that day? What do you think he'd think if he knew you were really a knight? Ho ho!"

Dinadan didn't answer. It was hardly ever necessary to answer Culloch's questions. Sir Kai closed his eyes in anguish. "How long did you promise to stay with this addlepate?" he asked Sir

Bedivere in a low voice.

"Until he's achieved knighthood or has given up trying," Bedivere said softly. He smiled ruefully at his cousin. "It may take longer than I thought."

"Not so long if I kill him," Sir Kai muttered.

Perhaps to change the subject, Sir Bedivere turned to Dinadan. "I liked the way you handled yourself at court last night, young Dinadan."

"What do you mean, Sir Bedivere?" Dinadan asked, blushing.

"Call me Bedivere. I meant the way that you downplayed your own victory before the king. Believe me, young knights are more likely to exaggerate their deeds than otherwise."

"I think I've already done that enough," Dinadan muttered. At Bedivere's questioning glance, he explained. "You see, I wrote that song about my victory myself."

Sir Kai glanced quickly at Dinadan, but the knight's eyes were unreadable. "Ah, yes," Bedivere said. "As you were travelling as a minstrel. So, in your retelling, you made yourself more heroic than you were?"

"Yes, but not for my own sake," Dinadan added hastily. "It just made for a better story the way I told it. That's all."

"So what really happened?" Bedivere asked

quietly. Dinadan told him. He meant to tell only the barest outline of the true story, but Bedivere listened intently and asked questions, so by the time he had done, Bedivere knew every detail. The knight said, "You did rather improve on the tale, didn't you?"

Dinadan nodded.

"But," Bedivere added, "you went back alone to face Sir Annui, only to help Sir Edmund. That argues considerable courage, which is much more knightly than mere skill with weapons. I don't think that Arthur made a mistake in admitting you to the table, do you, Kai?"

Sir Kai, who had had not looked at Dinadan during the story, but who had kept his horse within earshot, pursed his lips, then said abruptly, "I gather you're not any good with a sword."

Dinadan swallowed. "No, sir."

"Pity. But I suppose swordsmanship's not everything." With that, he kicked his horse and trotted ahead.

Bedivere chuckled. "You may not believe it, Dinadan, but that was Kai's way of showing approval."

"Then I hope I never see his disapproval."

"That would be too much to ask, lad," Bedivere said, still smiling. "Say, what's ahead?"

Culloch, who had ridden ahead, had come to a

halt at the top of the next hill, where he appeared to be talking with a stranger. As they drew near, Culloch laughed with delight and launched into a jumble of introductions. "My name is Culloch, and I'm going to be a great knight someday, so you'll want to remember that name, and these are my helpers, Kai and Bedivere and Stearnes."

The stranger to whom these words were addressed turned in his saddle, and Dinadan saw with sharp interest that he carried a lyre. "Is it indeed the Great Kai, slayer of kings, whom I see before me? It is an honour, sir." The stranger bowed as deeply as he could, but as he was short of stature and wide of girth and sitting in a saddle besides, this was not very low.

"Ay, my name's Kai," the knight said gruffly.

Without another word, the stranger slipped his lyre from his shoulder, strummed the strings once, then began to proclaim in a voice that was half singing, "'Tis Kai, the great, the mightiest of the mighty, who slew five kings with one fell blow —"

"Was it really five?" Dinadan whispered to Bedivere.

"Two," Bedivere replied, "and not in one blow either."

The strange minstrel continued, "— Kai, who can live nine days and nine nights under water without breathing, and who can stay nine days and nine nights awake without sleep. Kai, whose sword cleaves a wound that no physic can cure. Kai, who can be as tall as the tallest tree when he chooses, and whose anger burns so hot that he stays dry even in the heaviest rain. Kai, the great, the magnificent, the unmatched. Yea, my lords and ladies, 'tis Kai."

The minstrel bowed again and seemed to be expecting applause, but he was met with utter silence. At last Bedivere said, "Why, Kai, I believe you've been holding out on us."

Kai rolled his eyes. "He forgot to mention that I can start a fire by rubbing a stick on a minstrel's back. Shall I show you?"

Culloch, who had been frowning over the minstrel's paean to Kai, caught at least part of this speech. "A fire! And dinner! Yes, Kai, you are right. It is past dinnertime! Friend minstrel, will you join us? You are welcome to our camp and to our quest as well, if you like!"

Culloch swung down from his horse at once. After a quick exchange of glances, Bedivere and Kai joined him. The minstrel bowed again. "I am honoured too deeply for words."

"Well, that's something," said Sir Kai.

"I shall certainly join you on your quest. My name,"

the minstrel paused expressively, "is Wadsworth."

He appeared to expect the others to know the name, but clearly none did. Bedivere smiled a polite greeting, Dinadan nodded, and Kai muttered cryptically, "Yes, very likely."

Over the fire that night, Culloch found his knightly deed. Despite Wadsworth's claim to be speechless, he talked as incessantly as Culloch, and shortly after they had begun eating, the minstrel told Culloch about a wealthy king named Isbaddadon who lived just a day's journey to the west. "The king has just proclaimed that his own fair daughter Olwen must marry, but the knight who earns her hand has to prove himself first, by performing great tasks!"

Culloch's eyes lit up, but Bedivere said quietly, "I see no value in this, Culloch. King Arthur will be more pleased with deeds done to help the weak than with those done to win a bride for yourself."

"And besides," Dinadan added. "Do you really want to get married? You don't even know this Olwen. Chances are she's a fright."

"But what if she's beautiful?" Culloch said.

"Even worse," Dinadan replied promptly. "Surely you don't mean to be one of those pathetic men who always chase after pretty women, slave to each, despised by all?"

Sir Kai nodded curt approval at Dinadan, but Culloch was unconvinced. Nothing anyone could say had the least effect, and when he rolled over to sleep off his dinner, it was clear that he would take up King Isbaddadon's challenge.

The next morning, pausing only for an hour and a half for breakfast, Culloch was off, pushing his horse at a gruelling pace. Only the minstrel Wadsworth made any effort to keep up with him, and so it happened that Culloch was far ahead and well out of earshot when they heard a woman's cry for help. Bedivere pulled up sharply and looked about. "It came from the woods to the south," Dinadan said.

"Come on, then," Bedivere said, "and blast Culloch for riding ahead and missing his chance to do something of value." Bedivere spurred his horse into the thickets, followed by Sir Kai and Dinadan. A minute later they heard the woman's voice again, this time not calling for help but rather embarked on a furious and very eloquent tirade against someone.

As one, the three knights pulled up. "Are we going to help the woman or the person she's speaking to?" Dinadan asked mildly.

Kai grinned, and Bedivere replied, "Let's take a

look. In truth, it sounds as if this woman may be able to take care of herself."

They dismounted and crept forward through the woods. A moment later they came upon a strange scene. A lady in expensive but torn and dirty robes was tied to a tree. Two burly men, wearing the livery of castle guards, stood panting before her. One had long scratches on his face. It appeared that they had only that moment finished securing her and were resting from the exertion. The lady had long black hair, almost to her waist, and would have been quite pretty, but she was not at her best. Her face was smudged, and her hair wildly tangled. Moreover, she was embarked on the most eloquent denunciation of her captors – and of the entire race of men – that Dinadan had ever heard. From a purely artistic point of view, he had to acknowledge that she had a gift with language. The knights stopped behind a large gorse bush to watch.

"— and furthermore, you're ugly, even more so than most men. I suppose I ought to thank your master for being so thoughtful as to send two foul, rump-fed, tumour-ridden, pox-marked creatures to murder me. It almost makes me welcome death, to think that at least I shall no longer inhabit the same earth and breathe the same air as two such blisters as you!"

"My lady," one guard protested. "You know we didn't ask for this task. But you tried to poison our mistress!"

"Don't be an ass! She was my mistress, too! What would I gain by killing her?"

The other guard tried – unsuccessfully, in Dinadan's opinion – to look cunning, and said, "Ah, but you be a sorceress, they say. You could have dark schemes."

The lady rolled her eyes. "What a gudgeon! Look here, cod's head, if I were a sorceress, you would both be toads by now." She gasped suddenly. "Why, good heavens! You *are* toads! I must be a sorceress after all!"

The first guard rose. "Come on, Jem. Let's get it over with. Take her head off, and we can go home."

Bedivere coughed politely and stepped from behind the bush. The guards whirled around. "Pardon my intrusion, madam, but I feel compelled to interrupt. My good men, you will most certainly not kill this lady."

"Lady! She's a witch!"

Dinadan laughed, and he and Sir Kai followed Bedivere. "I daresay she is," Kai said. "You still can't kill her."

"Come now," Dinadan added, "if she were a

witch, could these ropes hold her?" Producing his hunting knife, Dinadan cut through the woman's bonds, and she lurched away from the tree.

"Watch out!" the guards shouted, taking several quick steps back. "She's dangerous!"

Bedivere put his hand on his sword. "If you or anyone else has a complaint about this woman, let it be taken to King Arthur's court, where we are knights of his Round Table."

At the knowledge that they faced Arthur's knights, the guards' belligerance dissolved. After a short mumbled apology, they backed away into the shrubbery, and a moment later Dinadan heard them mounting horses and riding away. Bedivere turned to the lady. "I hope you've come to no harm, my lady."

"Well, that's a fatuous thing to say," the lady snapped, rubbing her wrists. "Why don't you try being roped to a tree and see how you like it?"

Bedivere lifted one eyebrow, but lost none of his polish. "Indeed, my lady. Is there somewhere that we could conduct you where you might be safe?"

"I doubt it," the lady said, half to herself. "I suppose I should thank you for helping me anyway, even though it didn't take much to scare off those two louts."

"It seems to me, Bedivere," Dinadan said

thoughtfully, "that this gracious lady would rather be left alone. Shall we?"

"Peace, Dinadan. My lady, as we cannot be certain that those two have truly gone, I hope you will accept our offer of an escort from this place. My name is Bedivere, and these are Sir Dinadan and Sir Kai, both of King Arthur's Round Table."

The lady looked appraisingly at Bedivere and Kai, and sceptically at Dinadan, but at last she nodded. "I don't suppose I can refuse. My name is Brangienne."

They made room for Lady Brangienne on Dinadan's spare horse by dividing its load between them, then set out. She could tell them no place to take her, and so they resumed following Culloch. After all, Bedivere said, perhaps she would be safe at the castle of King Isbaddadon. The lady acquiesced grudgingly. "I don't see that I've gained much," she muttered. "I'm rid of two men, but now I'm stuck with three."

Bedivere smiled, still unruffled. "At least we shan't tie you to a tree, my lady."

"However much we may be tempted," added Dinadan. Lady Brangienne scowled blackly at Dinadan, who ignored her and took out his rebec. "Say, Bedivere, have I sung you my song about ladyhood yet? I wrote this one after I met the lovely Lady Miriam." Crossing his legs on his saddle, Dinadan tuned the rebec, then began.

> "A dragon from the swampy fen
> Became a wretched pest
> He ate most all the crops of men
> And set to fire the rest.

> "He burned the castle of a knight
> And stripped his storehouse bare.
> He drank the moat, then in the night,
> He stole his lady fair.

> "Alas! What woe! The knight did howl!
> A wretched choice! Alack!
> For if he slew the lizard foul,
> He'd get the lady back!

> "To fight a worm is doubly hard
> When equal evils cancel.
> Which one is better to discard?
> The dragon? Or the damsel?"

When Dinadan was done, Sir Kai's eyes wrinkled at
the corners, and even Bedivere's lips trembled, but
neither spoke. Dinadan smiled blandly at the lady.
That she was furious was clear, but Dinadan saw
something else in her eyes – a speculative curiosity.

Dinadan sat between Bedivere and Sir Kai at King Isbaddadon's long banquet table and folded his hands patiently. The ladies had not yet come to dinner, and courtly custom demanded that the men not eat until all were seated. King Isbaddadon, though, was less constrained by courtly custom and was already burrowing into his first plate of food. On Bedivere's other side, Culloch also restrained himself for the sake of manners, but he fidgeted and gazed longingly at the food. Dinadan sympathised with him. It did seem pointless to observe the niceties of correct behaviour before King Isbaddadon, who clearly regarded both polite behaviour and his knightly guests as bothersome matters he would as soon be rid of.

He seemed especially disturbed by Culloch, and every few moments, the king would look up from his platter to gaze balefully at his daughter's would-be suitor. He evidently did not consider Culloch a suitable match. Culloch seemed oblivious to his host's antipathy, though; his eyes never left his plate of food. As for Sir Kai, his eyes never left the king. Under his breath, he muttered to Bedivere. "I told you we should have brought our weapons to dinner."

"It would have been an insult, Kai. One doesn't arm oneself for a banquet."

"You think our host gives a groat for such scruples? You'll notice he brought a weapon." It was true. A long boar spear leaned conspicuously against the table at King Isbaddadon's right.

There was a rustle of drapes, and the ladies appeared at last. First came Lady Olwen, King Isbaddadon's daughter, then a bevy of ladies-in-waiting. Last of these was Lady Brangienne, who was now evidently a part of Lady Olwen's retinue. Dinadan noted this with mild surprise, but his eyes returned to Lady Olwen. It would have been hard to find a more unremarkable lady. She had a plain, round face that was made to look even rounder by her choice of hairstyle – two fat pigtails sticking out from each side of her head. She was short, even squat, and walked with neither grace nor assurance. From the contours of her figure, it was evident that she was a woman, but her expression was that of a child, and an uncommonly spoiled one at that. Dinadan glanced sharply at Culloch, who was proposing to endure great trials for the hand of this lady, but Culloch showed no surprise or regret or indeed anything else. As soon as the ladies had appeared, Culloch had turned his whole attention to eating.

"It seems that our companion has found a home here," Bedivere murmured in his ear. "I am not surprised. I guessed she had been a lady-in-waiting."

"Ladies-in-waiting are shrewish, are they?" Dinadan asked innocently. Bedivere shook his head, but did not reply, and the two applied themselves to their meals.

All who ate at the table finished at roughly the same time, even though some (Isbaddadon and Culloch) ate twice as much as the others. Dinadan noticed that Lady Olwen did justice to her dinner as well, but that the ladies-in-waiting ate nothing. At last the king rose and turned his attention to his guests.

"Well, Ollie!" he trumpeted to his daughter. "What d'ye think of your suitor?"

Lady Olwen simpered and blinked very rapidly at Culloch. The eyelid movement was apparently supposed to be flirtatious, but Dinadan found it oddly disconcerting. Culloch raised his cup and grinned foolishly.

"Blast it," Bedivere muttered. "The lad's fuddled."

"And he's even brought us a gift, a fine wench to be your lady-in-waiting!" Isbaddadon laughed without humour, and was joined by Culloch, who had come to the rollicking stage of his inebriation. The king bowed toward the lady in question and said, "Welcome, Lady Bragwaine."

The lady looked pained. "My lord, forgive me, but my name is Brangienne."

The king grunted. "One of those pothersome foreign names!" he announced, as if this explained something. He turned back toward Culloch, and his eyes grew hard. "But we can't give my gel away just because you gave us one, too. Can't swap a princess for a wench, now, can I? What can you offer me in exchange?" Culloch babbled something nearly incoherent, but the word "task" appeared several times, and King Isbaddadon snapped back, "Of course you'll do a task, as many as I ask! But I want something now! Tell us a tale, why don't you?"

Culloch hiccuped and grinned. Dinadan closed his eyes with anguish. Another cup and Culloch would be under the table.

"I said —"

Dinadan started to speak, but before he could say a word, a shrill voice interrupted from the servants' gallery. It was Wadsworth. "Your gracious highness! If I may, I shall speak for my master and shall tell thee a tale!"

King Isbaddadon glared at the minstrel, then shrugged. "Make it a good one, then, and your master lives." He leaned back in his chair and reached for another flagon of wine.

Wadsworth strummed his instrument, then said, "Because your lordship is here in Wales, I tell of a Welsh hero, and call upon all the Welsh heroes to witness my telling. I call upon Gwydden the Difficult, Sugyn son of Sugynedydd (who could suck up a sea in a draught), Cacamwri the Barn Flailer, Llong, Dygyvlong, Anoeth the Bold, Eiddyl the Tall, and Amren the Also Tall, Gwevyl son of Gwastad (whose lip drooped to his navel when he was sad), and Uchdryd Cross Beard."

"He's making this up, isn't he?" Dinadan whispered to Bedivere.

"Nay, lad," Bedivere replied. "Some of the old minstrels think it mightily impressive to show off their memory for names. Impressive, but dull."

King Isbaddadon appeared to agree. His scowl grew blacker at each new name. Nothing could slow Wadsworth, though. "Even more, I call upon Bolch, Kyvolch, and Syvolch, the three sons of Cleddych Kyvolch and the grandsons of Cleddyv Divolch, who had three swords named Glas, Glessig, and Gleisyad, and three dogs named Call, Cuall, and Cavall, and three horses named Hoyrddyddog, Drogddyddog, and Lloyrddyddog, and three wives named —"

Wadsworth got no further. With a roar, King Isbaddadon leaped to his feet and snatched up his boar spear. Dinadan stared, unable to move or even to think except to wonder whether the king would kill Culloch or Wadsworth first, but Sir Kai was much quicker. As fast as thought, he had thrown himself across the table toward King Isbaddadon. The king hurled his spear toward Culloch, but Sir Kai – Dinadan would have laughed at this if he'd heard it in a tale, but it happened nevertheless – Sir Kai caught the spear in midflight.

Everyone froze in astonishment, staring at the spear in Sir Kai's grasp. Even Sir Kai seemed hardly to believe it, but he reversed it in a flash and held the point an inch from Isbaddadon's nose. "It's not good manners to kill your guests," Sir Kai said.

"Guards!" shouted the king, and at once thirty men armed with longbows appeared from what had evidently been a planned ambush.

"And do you think your men can kill me before I split your skull?" Sir Kai asked. And then there was silence for a long moment, while Sir Kai and the king stared at each other, neither moving a muscle.

"I have an idea," Dinadan said suddenly, trying to keep his voice calm. "It seems that our host has already heard the fine tale that our friend Wadsworth told —"

"Actually, I hadn't even begun the —"

"Be quiet, fool!" Bedivere hissed at Wadsworth. "Go on, Dinadan."

"Thank you. But if I could tell a tale that was more to your liking, then perhaps you would be satisfied, your highness."

King Isbaddadon did not move his eyes from Sir Kai, but after a second, replied, "Agreed."

Dinadan licked his lips, took a breath, and began. Afraid that he would be too self-conscious singing the Tale of Sir Dinadan, he began the tale he had composed before leaving home, the story of Sir Tristram's battle with the evil knight Sir Marhault. Never had the telling of a tale come so hard to him. Not only did he not have his rebec, but the room was filled with tension. Dinadan's voice wavered nervously, but the spear that Sir Kai held in King Isbaddadon's face remained steady. When at last Dinadan finished, the hall was silent for a long moment, then King Isbaddadon nodded slowly.

"It was well told," he said at last. "You may go, guards."

Only when the last guard was gone did Sir Kai relax and move the spear point away from the king. King Isbaddadon stood. "I'll give your champion his first task in the morning," he announced and walked out of the room.

Sir Kai and Bedivere and Dinadan looked at

each other. "You might have told a shorter tale, lad," Sir Kai said gruffly, but his lips curled in what was almost a smile.

"Good Gog, Kai," Bedivere said. "You caught that spear in flight! I've never seen the like! They should write a song about that." Bedivere glanced inquiringly at Dinadan.

Dinadan shook his head. "Nobody would believe it."

Bedivere nodded. "In any case, Kai, you saved his life."

Sir Kai's smile faded as he glanced at Culloch, who had gone to sleep with his face in a sauce bowl during the story. "Don't remind me," Sir Kai said.

Judging by the stars, it was after midnight, but Dinadan was wide awake, his stomach complaining loudly that, in all the excitement, he had not eaten enough dinner. After vainly trying several times to go back to sleep, he gave up and rose from his bed to go hunting the kitchens.

It took a long time, feeling his way down strange hallways, but at last he found them, only to discover that someone had preceded him. Lady Brangienne was there, back to the door, hungrily devouring a chicken. Dinadan watched her a moment, then said mildly, "Don't take it all."

Lady Brangienne jumped and whirled around. Seeing Dinadan, the fear left her face and was replaced with intense dislike. "Oh, it's you."

Dinadan wondered at her scornful look, but he only asked, "Was there anything else where you got that chicken?" Lady Brangienne pointed to a partly open cabinet, where Dinadan saw some other cold meat. Nodding his thanks, he crossed the room and chose a half-eaten meat pie. Lady Brangienne never spoke, so at last Dinadan broke the silence. "You wouldn't be so hungry if you'd eat your dinner, you know."

Lady Brangienne snorted. "What dinner?" she snapped. "It's the custom here for Lady Olwen's ladies-in-waiting only to eat what is left over from my lady's plate."

"Sounds appetising," Dinadan said.

"Impossible, you mean. You may not have noticed, but she left nothing to speak of."

"Yes. I did see she had a good appetite."

Lady Brangienne snorted again. "All her other ladies make it a point to eat before dinner, but I didn't discover that until it was too late."

Dinadan smiled. "You should have left early. But then you'd have missed the excitement."

Lady Brangienne's eyes lit with anger. "Excitement! Slanderous lies, more like!" Dinadan blinked and stepped back involuntarily. "You and your fancy Sir Tristram! What do you know about Tristram anyway?"

"More than you might think!" Dinadan retorted.

"Did you see him kill Sir Marhault?"

"No," Dinadan returned promptly. "Did you?"

Lady Brangienne hesitated, then nodded. "Yes, I did. And it was nothing like your tale."

Dinadan stared, his anger overcome for the moment by his curiosity. "What happened?"

Lady Brangienne's eyes narrowed, and she glared at Dinadan. "Why do you care? You have your story already."

"You may believe that I want to know what really happened," Dinadan said softly.

Lady Brangienne still looked suspicious, but at length she began.

"I used to be chief lady to Queen Iseult, daughter of good King Aguissance of Ireland. We reached womanhood together, and no two ladies could have been closer than we two. Iseult grew as beautiful as her mother had been before her, and soon all the land called her La Belle Iseult.

"Iseult's mother was from Cornwall, the daughter of the impoverished King of Tintagel. When she and Aguissance were wed, the poor king could not even provide a dowry, and so he and Aguissance arranged for Tintagel to pay a small yearly tribute, and every year that sum was paid gladly. It was received gladly, too, because the King of Tintagel always sent the payment by the hand of his cousin, the great knight Sir Marhault."

Lady Brangienne glared again at Dinadan, but when he did not respond, resumed her story. "Those were the best times of the year. Aguissance loved Sir Marhault as a brother, and when he arrived there was feasting and hunting and jousting and all sorts of revelry. There was no one so kind, so brave, or so courteous as Marhault – a man who could look a king in the eye as an equal but who still took time to speak to young ladies-in-waiting." Lady Brangienne hesitated, her mind far away, in a different day.

Then she came back to the present and her voice hardened as she continued. "One year, though, Marhault arrived empty-handed. The old king had died, and his nephew, Mark, had assumed the throne. King Mark declared that he would no longer pay tribute and dared King Aguissance to send a champion if he cared to dispute it. Marhault was ashamed at having been sent with such a churlish message, and he asked the king if he could be Aguissance's champion himself. After some persuasion, Aguissance agreed."

"Hang on, I'm getting confused here," Dinadan said. "Sir Marhault was related to this King Mark, wasn't he?"

"Remotely, yes," Lady Brangienne replied.

"But he wanted to go back and challenge King Mark on behalf of the King of Ireland?"

"He was more at home with us than in Cornwall, he always said. And besides, as I just said, he was offended by King Mark's boorishness."

Dinadan nodded, and Lady Brangienne continued. "A combat was arranged between Sir Marhault and King Mark's champion, a young man named Sir Tristram. All the court travelled to Cornwall for the test, and I went with them. It was terrible, and all so stupid. The battle was supposed to be a test of skill, not a fight to the death, but Tristram never let up. We could all see that he meant to kill Marhault, and if Marhault had been a lesser knight he would have been in great danger."

"Wasn't he killed then?" Dinadan asked in surprise.

"Not fairly!" Lady Brangienne snapped. "After a long time, Marhault succeeded in disarming Tristram and knocking him down, but he refused to follow up his advantage and kill him while Tristram was defenceless. Instead, he turned away, thinking that the battle was over. Tristram grabbed up his sword and attacked again. Marhault died there, with Tristram's sword in his skull."

Dinadan swallowed. He wanted to believe that Lady Brangienne was lying, but her low voice carried deep conviction. His brother Tristram had killed a good man by attacking him from behind.

More quietly, Lady Brangienne continued. "Later we learned that King Mark had told Tristram it was a fight to the death, but it made no difference. Marhault was dead, and nothing has been right in either Ireland or Cornwall since."

Her voice faded, and she looked at the floor for a long time. At last Dinadan said, "I'm sorry. I didn't know. I had heard only that Tristram won the battle, and I made up the rest. I shouldn't have."

Lady Brangienne did not look up, but at last, she said, "At least it made for a good enough tale to save your lives tonight." A tear rolled down her cheek, and she dashed it away angrily with the back of her hand.

Dinadan looked away from her grief. "All the same," he said. "I won't tell it again."

4

SIR TRISTRAM

The sun was already high in the sky when Dinadan awoke, and he looked bemusedly around the unfamiliar room, remembering where he was. He was at the castle of King Isbaddadon, in the room he shared with Culloch, who was to be getting a task this morning in his quest to win the hand of the unappealing Olwen. Dinadan glanced at Culloch's bed, across the chamber, then sat up. Culloch was gone, along with his armour and weapons.

Ten minutes later, Dinadan was dressed and hurrying down the hallway. Since he did not know where he might find Culloch, he made his way towards the kitchens. It was as likely a guess as any, and there at least he could find some breakfast. But first he found Lady Brangienne.

She was just leaving the kitchens, carrying a scarf filled with baked goods. She lifted one eyebrow at Dinadan. "You're still here?" she asked abruptly. "I thought you'd gone with the others."

"They've gone?" Dinadan blinked. He couldn't believe Bedivere would leave without telling him.

"Of course," Lady Brangienne replied. "They've gone off to do Culloch's first task, if you can call it that."

Her voice was rich with scorn, and Dinadan looked at her inquiringly. "What do you mean? What's the task?"

"Don't you know?" Dinadan shook his head, and Lady Brangienne tossed her hair back out of her eyes with a sharp gesture that managed to communicate impatience and disdain at once. "The king has sent Culloch to plough his north field with two oxen. One of them has to be yellow and the other one spotted."

Dinadan's mouth dropped open. "You're joking," he said.

"I don't see why you're so shocked."

"Because it's stupid, of course. What good is —?"

"I don't see that it's more stupid than fighting another knight just to prove a point. As far as I can see, it's typical. Men! Knights! I've no patience with them." She tossed her hair back from her face

72

again and stalked away down the hall.

Dinadan let her go and continued to the kitchens. While he ate a slab of bread and butter and drank some ale, he pondered Lady Brangienne's information. He understood now why Bedivere had not bothered him – not only was the task silly and demeaning, but it would not take very long. That question resolved, Dinadan amused himself by imagining Sir Kai's feelings concerning this "knightly task".

He soon saw for himself. Shortly after noon, Culloch returned, driving two oxen, one of them coated and the other spattered with yellow paint. Behind them rode a weary Bedivere and a glowering Sir Kai. King Isbaddadon happened to be in the courtyard when the small procession arrived. He guffawed loudly. "Odd's blood, boy! Where did you get that paint?"

Dinadan was standing nearby, but he didn't wait to hear Culloch's story. He strolled back to where Bedivere and Sir Kai sat on their horses. Bedivere greeted him with a faint smile. "Hello, lad. Sorry we left you behind this morning."

Dinadan glanced back over his shoulder at the cattle. "No need to apologise. I'd as soon not go on a fool's errand."

Sir Kai snorted. "Any errand our Culloch is sent

on will be that."

"Maybe the second task will have more value," Bedivere said quietly. Sir Kai shook his head and scowled, and Dinadan could tell that even Bedivere didn't believe it.

They were right. Culloch's second task, received that evening, was to seek out and bring back a legendary magic goblet called the "Cup of Lloyr." They received the task in the banquet room, King Isbaddadon having decreed that every successful task should be celebrated by a feast. At first, Bedivere had been interested.

"Tell us more of this cup, your highness," he asked the king. "I have not heard of it before."

"It is an old tale of the Waleis people, and so you should begin your search in Wales."

Bedivere nodded and continued, "But what is the magical nature of this cup?" King Isbaddadon's brow furrowed, and Bedivere explained. "I mean does it have healing properties? Can it cure any ill? Right any wrong?"

King Isbaddadon roared with laughter. "Ay, it can do all that!" He laughed a moment longer, then said, a strange gleam in his eyes, "It is said that any wine drunk from this cup becomes the finest vintage and is stronger than any wine on earth!"

Bedivere closed his eyes, and Sir Kai muttered

an oath, but Culloch's face lit up. "Now I call that something useful!"

Culloch, Bedivere, Sir Kai, and Dinadan left the next morning, accompanied (to the displeasure of everyone but Culloch) by Wadsworth the minstrel. As they rode, Wadsworth hummed to himself a painfully simple melody with a short, four-stress line – Dah-de-Dah-de-Dah-de-Dah-de – over and over. Sir Kai had looked fit for murder since they set out, but when he actually moved his hand to rest on his sword hilt, Dinadan judged it was time to intervene. "Wadsworth, my friend," he said. "As you are accompanying our hero on his, ah, noble quest, it seems fitting that you should write the song of his adventures."

Wadsworth looked at Dinadan coldly and sniffed. "Why, I'm sure I could not do it so well as your lordship," he said, his lips prim. Dinadan stifled a grin. So Wadsworth still smarted from his story's poor reception, and Dinadan's success, back at Isbaddadon's court.

"But of course you could," Dinadan replied soothingly.

"To be quite honest," Wadsworth said, "heroic tales are not my real strength. I am far more skilled at love songs."

"Why then, you should write a love song for Culloch," Dinadan said promptly. "After all, these tasks of his are performed for the love of the fair Olwen, aren't they, Culloch?"

"Eh?" Culloch replied, surprised. Dinadan innocently repeated his question, and Culloch stammered back, "Ah, yes. Why, by Jove, yes they are, aren't they?"

Wadsworth peered closely at Dinadan. "Do you ever write love songs?"

"I've never written one."

"Then I challenge you! A duel of songsters! Each of us shall compose a song on Culloch's love for Olwen, and these knights shall judge between us!"

Dinadan felt a stir of pity for the old minstrel. Surely it must have been galling to have been shown up by a youth of Dinadan's age – who wasn't even really a minstrel. Resolving to compose a truly dreadful lyric so that Wadsworth could easily win, Dinadan agreed. Sir Kai then spoke suddenly. "This is an excellent plan for passing our time, but to make sure that each song is original, let us separate. Wadsworth, you ride ahead with Culloch – out of earshot, mind – and Dinadan stay with us."

It was the most pleasant part of the day. Dinadan took up his rebec and occasionally even played a few desultory notes and idly experimented with a few rhymes, but mostly he chatted with Bedivere. Even Sir Kai, away from Culloch and Wadsworth, thawed somewhat and became almost agreeable. Meanwhile, a quarter of a mile ahead on the path, they could see Wadsworth assiduously working at his lyre. Wadsworth must have taken the contest very seriously, because he worked at his song for almost four hours before at last he signalled his readiness to present the fruit of his efforts, and the two groups came together.

"Is your lordship ready?" the minstrel said.

"Whenever you are, friend Wadsworth," Dinadan said. "Shall I go first?"

Dinadan had offered out of generosity, feeling that it would be an advantage to go last, but Wadsworth's eyes narrowed with suspicion, and the minstrel launched into a long explanation of why it would be best for Dinadan to go last. Bored by Wadsworth's explanations, Dinadan agreed.

"My lords and ladies," Wadsworth began, assuming a formal tone.

"Ladies?" growled Sir Kai.

"I sing for you a melody of great love, the love of the noble Sir Culloch for his absent lady, the fair Olwen, for whom his soul longs, in whose memory his very breath moistens the air, and for whom his eyes stream tears." Here the minstrel paused, as if holding back tears himself.

"Off to a good start, eh?" Culloch asked cheerfully. "The next part's even better. I like the bit when he says —"

"Peace, Culloch," interrupted Bedivere. "Let the minstrel sing his own song."

Wadsworth continued. "The song is called, 'My Lief Is Faren in Londe,' which is to say, 'My love is far away.'"

"Then why the deuce don't you say it?" muttered Sir Kai, but at a look from Bedivere, he lapsed into silence. Without further introduction, Wadsworth began:

> *"My lief is faren in londe,*
> *Alas, why did I go?*
> *The cuckoo sings my song,*
> *'Jug jug, pu-we, to-witta-woo.'*
>
> *"I travel far and wide,*
> *Great deeds for love to do,*
> *But I, like the cuckoo, cry,*
> *'Jug jug, pu-we, to-witta-woo.'*
>
> *"Some day shall I be home*

To gaze her eyes into?
I'll whisper as I come,
'Jug jug, pu-we, to-witta-woo.'"

When the minstrel finished, there was a long silence. Dinadan carefully avoided looking at Bedivere or Sir Kai, but he could not doubt what they were thinking – "This took all afternoon?"

"See why I like it?" Culloch said heartily. "I like the last part best, when I whisper that thing."

"Jug jug witta poo poo," Sir Kai supplied.

"Jug jug, pu-we, to-witta-woo," Wadsworth corrected, giving Sir Kai a condescending smile.

"Ah. My mistake," Sir Kai said with a solemn nod.

Wadsworth turned to Dinadan, triumph in his eyes. "Now, shall we hear what his lordship has prepared?"

With a shrug, Dinadan swung his leg around and settled himself comfortably in the saddle with his rebec. He played a few bars, then began playing the same annoying little four-beat melody that Wadsworth had been humming earlier. He raised his voice and sang with a quavering vibrato:

"Great Culloch can be brave and gay
Throughout the sunlit hours of day.
But when upon his bed he lies,

Why then, for Olwen fair he cries.

"He sees her face, her pigtail stout,
The freckles sprinkled on her snout.
Then from his chest he heaves a sob,
And in his throat there grows a gob.

"He weeps; his pillow sogs with tears;
It oozes up around his ears.
The flowing trickle from his nose
Doth stain his face and cake his clothes.

"Because he mourns the absent Ollie,
Doth Culloch nobly grieve, by golly."

Bedivere and Sir Kai did not speak, both shaking with suppressed mirth, but Culloch frowned. "Not meaning anything harsh, of course, Stearnes, but I didn't care for that one all that much."

Wadsworth's chin lifted. "If I might make a suggestion, lad, it was not seemly to use the familiar name 'Ollie' in your poem."

"Couldn't hatch a rhyme for Olwen," Dinadan explained. "But I'm sure you're right."

"I could give you some other pointers sometime," the minstrel suggested.

Dinadan forced a smile. "You'd be wasting your

time, I'm afraid. I could never have written a song like yours." Wadsworth graciously accepted his victory, and Culloch began to talk about stopping for dinner.

Dinadan rolled over from his afternoon nap, stretched, then took up his rebec to play idly while he shook off the heavy feeling that came from sleeping during the day. He felt a twinge of guilt that he had not spent the day seeking the Cup of Lloyr, but it was only a twinge, and it passed quickly.

It was now three days since Culloch's search party had split up. After a while of asking everyone they met for the cup and receiving only puzzled stares, they had concluded that the quest would be more easily accomplished if they searched separately. They had set a place at which to meet again in three weeks' time, and then, to the relief of most of the party, had divided up. Dinadan, for his part, had asked two or three people he met if they had heard of the Cup of Lloyr, but recently he had been forgetting to ask. To be frank, the quest had begun to bore him.

When he was fully awake, he loaded up his horses and started off through the woods. He was looking for an inn where he might sing for his supper, but instead he found a knight, and a more majestic knight Dinadan had never seen, sitting still – almost as if posed – on a small hill, resplendent in gold-coloured armour.

"Good morrow, friend," Dinadan called out pleasantly. The knight's visored helm moved slightly, so that the knight could see, but otherwise there was no response. "Well met," Dinadan said. At last the knight's helm nodded slightly, then returned to its former position. Dinadan shrugged and rode on, but a few minutes later he pulled up at the sound of hoofbeats behind. The golden knight was following. Dinadan waited for him to catch up.

"Pleasant day, isn't it?" Dinadan said.

The knight sighed loudly. "If you wish."

"I didn't have anything to do with it," Dinadan pointed out. "My name's Dinadan. And you are — ?"

"I am a wandering knight, driven far from my home, where the love of my life is denied me by a cruel tyrant."

Dinadan nodded. "Bad luck," he said sympathetically.

"My love is the most beautiful lady in the world. I shall never be happy when I am away from her, and so I have sworn a vow of silence. I shall never again speak of her or of my love for her or of my grief."

"Won't you?" Dinadan asked. "Very... very noble, I'm sure."

"Perhaps, but I think nothing of that. It is only that there is no gain for me in uttering words that can only give me pain."

"Just so."

"To speak of the gold of her flaxen hair, to tell of the blue of her eyes, to express my love for her, than which there has never been such a love in all the history of man, cannot help me but rather can only harm me."

"You are quite right," Dinadan said. "Shall we ride in silence, then?"

"It would be to tear open my wound yet again, for every word I speak of her is as a red coal pressed to my breast, searing me to the very heart. I cannot speak her name. Nay, I cannot even speak my own, for to tell my own name is to speak of her, for what is Tristram but the slave of Iseult?"

Dinadan felt a chill in his heart, and he found himself unable to look at his companion. Was this fellow his brother? No, it couldn't be. After all, wouldn't his brother Tristram have recognised him – or at least recognised the name when Dinadan had introduced himself. "Are you really Sir Tristram?" he asked timidly.

"Who told you so?" the gold knight demanded.

"You did. Just now." The knight was silent, and Dinadan continued. "The same Sir Tristram who killed Sir Marhault?"

"The same."

"The son of Sir Meliodas of the Fens?"

This time the knight did not reply at once. "How came you to know that?" he asked.

"I am... I am somewhat acquainted with your family. I know your father and your brother."

"Brother?"

"Your younger brother."

Again Tristram hesitated, then straightened suddenly. "Why yes! I did have a brother! A paltry, skinny waif of no skill and no promise. I do remember! How do you know my father?"

Dinadan took a slow breath and looked at the empty forest ahead of him. "It doesn't matter," he said. "You should be keeping your vow of silence, after all."

Tristram agreed with this plan, at some length. He appeared to be much more impressed with the dramatic effect of taking a vow than he was with the inconvenience of keeping it. He may as well have kept it, though; Dinadan did not listen.

He could not explain why it so distressed him to meet his brother again and find him less than he had expected. It wasn't as if he had ever been close to Tristram or, for that matter, had ever had anything to do with him at all, except to admire him from afar. Nevertheless, when he thought back on his earlier self and remembered his childhood fantasies of one day riding side by side with his glorious brother, going on quest together, he writhed inside. It had all come true, after a fashion, but this fatuous clodpole beside him, jabbering incessantly about his noble vow of silence, had not been a part of that daydream.

"Hold!" Tristram said suddenly, pulling up abruptly. "Seest thou that knight? Is he not well-portioned?"

Dinadan glanced ahead of them, where a knight sat at the foot of a tree, holding a daisy and looking very abstractedly at the ground between his knees. "I couldn't say, Sir Tristram. Which portion did you mean?"

"It is a goodly knight. I shall salute him."

"What if he won't talk? I mean, maybe he's taken a vow of silence or something."

Tristram noticed no irony. "Then I shall respect his vow, of course. After all, it is the same vow I have taken myself. Good morrow, friend knight! Beest thou friend or foe?"

The knight looked up dreamily, and seeing Tristram and Dinadan approach, blinked once or twice. His face lost a touch of its dreaminess. "I am a friend to all lovers," he replied slowly, "and enemy to all who scorn love."

Tristram took a sharp breath. "Why then, you and I are of one soul indeed! For I am the same as you, and as two men struck by love, we breathe with but one breath. Though I know not your name, I know that I am closer to you than I am to my own brother."

Dinadan's lips twisted wryly. "It's true," he commented. "He really is."

The strange knight stood. "Then come to my arms," he exclaimed. "I am Sir Lamorak de Gales, knight of King Arthur's table and slave to the most beautiful woman in the world."

Tristram had swung off his mount and started forward, but at this last word froze in his tracks. "Indeed, it cannot be so. For I, Sir Tristram of Cornwall, love the most beautiful woman in the world, the Belle Iseult."

Sir Lamorak looked squarely at Tristram. "I have heard of you, and indeed have long wished to meet with you and call you brother, but this is not the meeting I had dreamed of."

"There's a lot of that going around," Dinadan said.

No one paid any attention, and Sir Lamorak continued, "For though I love thee, I will allow no man to stain the reputation of my fairy love. No earthly woman can match her."

"That we shall see," Tristram said through gritted teeth. He drew his sword, and Sir Lamorak immediately followed suit. Dinadan realised with incredulity that the two knights were going to fight over whose lady was prettier.

"Wait half a minute," he interjected. "What about all that business about being a friend to all lovers and breathing the same soul and all that rot? You aren't really going to fight, are you?"

"Sir Tristram may retract his words," Sir Lamorak said. "Else I am sworn to defend my lady to the death."

"As am I," said Tristram. "I mean, as you may also retract also your… your words, also, I mean not also but instead of me. Then, then also sworn am I to…"

It did not appear to Dinadan that Tristram was going to extricate himself from his speech, and so he turned his mount's head and rode on down the path, leaving the two knights behind. A moment later he heard the clang of swords, but before long he had ridden out of hearing, and he was alone again.

Two and a half weeks later, at the appointed meeting place, Dinadan rejoined Culloch, Bedivere, Sir Kai, and Wadsworth. To Dinadan's considerable surprise – and evidently also to that of Bedivere and Kai – Culloch bore with him the fabled Cup of Lloyr. It was a simple wooden flagon on which had been roughly carved the letters LLOYR. Looking closely, Dinadan thought that the carving looked altogether too recent for this cup to be of very great age. He glanced quickly at Bedivere and Sir Kai. "Was, ah, was either of you with Culloch when he achieved his prize?"

Bedivere shook his head slowly, his eyes meeting Dinadan's quizzical glance with a look of weariness. Sir Kai, standing beside Dinadan, said gruffly, "I'm sure you shall hear the tale soon. Until then, keep your thoughts to yourself, lad. You would not wish to prolong this quest, would you?"

Sir Kai was right. Even if the cup was fake, what would be the value of pointing it out? Dinadan heard the tale that very night, but the story did not make anything more clear, as Wadsworth's telling included such details as Culloch's fighting off three giants and leaping over tall pine trees and hurling rocks as large as cows. If anything, the fanciful account made things worse, because Dinadan could not believe that King Isbaddadon would accept either the tale or the cup as genuine.

He was wrong. Either King Isbaddadon was not very observant, or he didn't care, because when they had returned to the king's home with the "Cup of Lloyr" the king only ordered the cooks to prepare a banquet. As for Wadsworth's tale, Isbaddadon's only response to it was to laugh uproariously and clap Culloch heavily on the back a few times. Culloch, his face buried in a plate of boar meat, sauce dripping in globs from his chin, hardly seemed to notice. Bedivere held his head in his hands and looked old. Dinadan looked away with distaste, and his eyes met Lady Brangienne's. She was gazing steadily at Dinadan and was not at all embarrassed when Dinadan noticed her stare. She nodded gravely at him, and Dinadan nodded back. He didn't like her, of course, but he needed to be civil; he wanted to ask her a few questions later.

Dinadan didn't know when he'd find her alone, though. King Isbaddadon was supposed to give Culloch his next task the following morning, and then they would be off again. Luck was with him, though. At midnight, his lack of appetite at dinner having caught up with him, he made his way to the kitchens and found her waiting there.

"Well, it's about time you got here."

"Did we have an appointment?" Dinadan asked, surprised.

"Not officially, but when else were we to talk?"

"Are we having a secret tryst, my lady? Because

I'll have you know I'm not that sort —"

"Don't be an ass," Lady Brangienne said impatiently. "Where the devil did you dig up that silly cup? Any fool could see it's a fake. Aren't the knights of the Round Table supposed to be honourable and trust-worthy or something like that?"

"We knights of the table had nothing to do with it," Dinadan snapped back, nettled. "That was all Culloch's doing, while we were looking for the cup separately."

Lady Brangienne digested this information for a moment, then said, "Yes, I can see that. Whatever your numerous faults, you aren't a fool, and only a fool would try to pass that off as an ancient cup. But still, I didn't notice you objecting to the fraud."

Dinadan shook his head slowly. "I think it bothers Bedivere more than he shows. But as for Sir Kai and me, you're right: we don't object at all. Answer me this: is it worse to end a stupid task falsely or to continue a stupid task honestly?"

Lady Brangienne paused, considering this. At last, a tiny smile beginning at the corner of her mouth, she said, "It's a close race, isn't it? All right, I suppose I understand, even if I don't like it. I'm glad you and Bedivere didn't plan it, anyway."

She started to leave, but Dinadan held up his

hand and touched her sleeve. "Wait!"

Lady Brangienne looked at Dinadan's hand for a second. "Yes?"

"I need to ask you something. Didn't you say that Sir Marhault was killed fighting for the King of Ireland and his daughter Iseult?"

"That's right." Her face grew forbidding at the memory.

"And Tristram killed him, right?"

"That's what I said. Why are you — ?"

"So why is Tristram in love with Iseult?"

Lady Brangienne looked carefully at Dinadan. "How did you hear that?"

"Tristram told me himself. I ran into him while I was out."

"He told you?" Lady Brangienne rolled her eyes. "He is *such* a moron." She frowned suddenly. "You didn't mention me to him, did you?" Dinadan shook his head, and she let out a breath. "Good. Don't. I don't want him to know where I am." And with that, she turned on her heels and strode briskly away, leaving Dinadan alone, more confused than ever.

5

QUESTING

Culloch's next task, which was announced the following morning, was much like the one before. He was to seek out and find the Magic Picnic Basket of Guidno, which could miraculously refill itself as soon as it was emptied, so that no picnic party should ever be short of food. Culloch's eyes had gleamed at the very thought. Bedivere had pleaded with King Isbaddadon to assign a task that would actually help someone in need, but it was no use; and leaving behind the minstrel Wadsworth, who had caught a chill, the four rode away. Sir Kai was disgusted, Bedivere despondent, Culloch delighted, and Dinadan preoccupied. His mind was busy with something besides the search for the perfect picnic.

For Dinadan had his own quest now. There was

some mystery surrounding his brother Tristram and the Irish princess Iseult, and that mystery somehow touched on the person of Lady Brangienne, who wished it kept secret. He was not sure why he felt compelled to discover the truth, but he intended to find it nevertheless. The only place he could think of to investigate was in Cornwall, where King Mark held court at Tintagel Castle, and where most of the stories about Tristram took place. So, as soon as the knights were out of sight of Isbaddadon's castle, Dinadan suggested that they separate again, and when the others agreed, he headed in that direction. After all, he reflected, there were probably as many magic picnic baskets in Cornwall as there were anywhere else. He'd try to remember to ask around.

They were short on magic baskets in Cornwall, it seemed, but Dinadan had no trouble locating Tristram. Nearly everyone had heard of the great, love-lorn knight in golden armour who would not reveal his name because of a vow. Surely there was never a knight that travelled incognito so publicly. And so it was that after only five days of searching, Dinadan rode up to a stone hermitage in the woods, where a harried-looking young Benedictine monk greeted him and, when asked if he knew Tristram, jerked his head at the stone building and said, "Inside. You can take him with you, if you want."

Dinadan grinned. "I see. Has he been vowing silence at you?"

The monk sighed. "He never stops. Heaven help women everywhere if he should take a vow of chastity." Dinadan laughed aloud, but the monk frowned and shook his head briskly. "Oh bother, I've done it again. I'm supposed to be learning patience in my solitude, and there I go snipping at someone."

"Don't let it worry you," Dinadan said, swinging down from his horse. "I'm sure your patience has been well exercised since Tristram arrived. How long has he been here, by the way?"

"More than a week," the monk said. "Almost as long as I have." Dinadan looked a question, and the monk explained. "My name is Brother Eliot, from St Anselm's Abbey up the road. This little anchorage is a part of the abbey. We monks get sent here sometimes to pray and fast and meditate and so on when we need... need to be reminded of the seriousness of our calling. I got two weeks this time."

Dinadan chuckled. "Got a bit frivolous, did you?"

"It's not that," Brother Eliot said. "It's just that Father Abbot is a very... a very properly mournful father, and he dislikes it when the brothers appear to be enjoying their tasks too much."

"And what is your task?"

"I'm one of the junior cantors – a musician."

Dinadan's smile broadened. "Are you really?" he said, patting his rebec where it hung from his saddle. "We shall have to sing together. But first, I need to talk to your guest."

Brother Eliot's face lit up, and he said, "He was asleep just a moment ago. Is that a rebec?" Dinadan nodded, and the monk said, "I have only seen one, but it made such a sweet sound, I have never forgotten it." He looked eagerly at Dinadan, who needed no further prompting. He took the instrument down, tuned it quickly, then played a wistful melody he had been working on during his rides alone. Brother Eliot closed his eyes and shivered with bliss. When Dinadan was done, there were tears in the monk's eyes, and he took several long breaths before he spoke. "I wish... I wish..."

"What do you wish?"

Brother Eliot looked down guiltily. "It is nothing. I am a very young brother, and there are many things that I do not understand, but I... I do not see why we have no such instruments in the choir. Surely such beauty would be best used in praise of God. How much better it would be to play such music to a sacred song than it is to play it with tales of bloodshed and wrath!"

Dinadan pursed his lips. "You mean, like in stories of knights?" Brother Eliot nodded, and

Dinadan said mildly, "But I *like* stories of knights."

Brother Eliot looked guilty again. "Yes, there is a certain... pleasure.... But think of what good could be done! Why, imagine if the minstrels who sang of Sir Gawain should turn their talents in praise of the noble defenders of the church in the Holy Lands!"

"Who?" Dinadan asked.

"The Crusaders! They who fight and die to recover the Holy City Jerusalem from the infidel in faraway lands!"

"Why?" Dinadan asked. Brother Eliot looked confused, and Dinadan added, "I mean, why do they want Jerusalem?"

"It's... it's the Holy City. Where Our Lord walked. We good Christians must defend it, of course."

"Oh," Dinadan said, his mind suddenly focused on an idea for a verse. Brother Eliot started to speak, but Dinadan shushed him. "Hang on a minute, I think I have a song for you." He fingered the strings for a moment, words dancing in his head, and then he straightened. "Right, then. A song for the Crusaders. Ready?"

Brother Eliot nodded eagerly, and Dinadan ran the bow over the rebec's strings and sang:

> "What must the infidel have thought,
> Beholding those corsairs?
> How bravely the Crusaders fought

For lands that were not theirs.

"How utterly, completely mad
To fly to the defence
Of cities they had never had
And haven't wanted since."

Brother Eliot was quiet for a moment, then said softly, "Perhaps the Crusades are not the best subject after all, friend... I'm sorry, I don't even know your name."

"Dinadan. And I'm sorry to make light of your idea. It was ill done of me, but once the idea had started, I could hardly stop. I'm afraid that I, at least, could never write convincingly about the Crusades."

"Never mind," Brother Eliot said. "Will you stay with me tonight and share my meal? It is nothing but thin soup and water, a penitent's meal, but all I have is yours." He smiled, but the smile faded slightly. "Except, of course, what Sir Tristram eats."

Dinadan grinned. "Let Sir Tristram have the soup. I have some food in my pack left from my noontime meal at an inn down the road. There's some roast chicken and two good loaves of bread. It may not be a penitent's meal, but it's a meal you can give thanks for."

Brother Eliot hesitated, but not for long. He

nodded agreement, and Dinadan took out his feast, more than enough for both to eat well. Brother Eliot stared.

"I really shouldn't," he said. "When we come out to the anchorage, we're supposed to put aside all venial pleasures." He sighed. "That's always been the hardest part for me. Not obedience, not poverty, not chastity – but I do like good food and music, and I've never been able to see them as entirely corrupt. But I must trust Father Abbot, I suppose." He sighed and then, clearly putting Father Abbot out of his mind, laid into the chicken.

When their meal was over, Brother Eliot lay on his back and chewed on a piece of grass. "Are you a minstrel?" he asked suddenly.

"Sometimes," Dinadan replied.

"Do you sing short songs mostly, or do you write knightly tales?"

"Mostly tales," Dinadan said.

Brother Eliot ruminated for a minute, then cast a sidelong glance at Dinadan. "You know, I've had an idea for a knightly tale."

This was said so guiltily that Dinadan was hard put not to laugh. "And you a monk!" he said with mock horror.

"Oh, this would be a religious tale," Brother Eliot assured him, adding hastily, "and it's not about the Crusades, either, so don't give me that look. It's a story about a knight fighting great battles, but it would really be about faith."

Dinadan had a feeling he would regret asking, but he said, "How would that be?"

"It would be an allegory!" Brother Eliot continued eagerly. "Everything in the tale would really stand for something else! The hero would be a true Christian. I'd call him the Knight of the Cross – no, that's been used, hasn't it? – the Red Cross Knight. There, that's good. And the Red Cross Knight would fight against all sorts of sins and temptations."

"So he'd fight against a dragon named Gluttony, or something like that?" Dinadan asked.

"Well, yes, that's the idea, but I don't think the names should be that obvious. We'd have to call the dragon something else."

"We could call him Culloch," Dinadan said, musing.

"No, no. Let me explain. The hearer should be able to figure it out, but not easily. How about 'Grandmangeur' – from the French for 'big eater'. You see?"

"No," Dinadan said bluntly. "If you want people to understand the hidden meaning, then why hide it in the first place?"

"It's hard to explain, but that's just how it's done," Brother Eliot explained patiently. "I'd have the Red Cross Knight fighting for the deliverance of a beautiful woman who would be the one true faith. I'd call her 'Singulette'. For 'One', you know."

Dinadan made a face. "Ugh. Sounds like an undergarment. Can't you just call her One Faith?"

Brother Eliot shook his head impatiently. "You really need to read some of the writings of the Church Fathers. You've no notion how allegory works. You can't call her what you want her to represent. You call her something that will make your reader think of the word you want her to represent. I'll call her Una."

Dinadan started to speak, then closed his mouth and frowned in puzzlement.

"Look, it's simple," Brother Eliot said. "Suppose I want to have a knight who represents Foolishness. Well, I can't call him Fool."

"Yes, I see that. He'd hate it."

"No, no, I mean that would be too obvious. What we want is a name that will imply Fool."

"How about 'Tristram'?"

"Hush. Now we might disguise the word, maybe by turning it backwards."

"Loof? Sir Loof? 'The Ballad of Sir Loof'?"

Brother Eliot suppressed a grin, but shook his

head. "Not the right feel. So we might use a word that means foolishness in another language. Do you know how to say 'fool' in French?"

"No."

Brother Eliot sighed. "Me neither. Well, there's always Latin – that's *stultus*." He smiled sheepishly. "At least that's what the Latin master always calls me. So he could be Sir Stultus." He frowned and fell into a reverie. "Or, if that's too obvious, we could turn that one about – Sir Sutluts. Or what about Greek?"

Dinadan interrupted good-humouredly. "I really don't think I have the knack of saying things by pretending to say something else. I just like to tell stories. You'll have to find someone else to write your allegory, and give him my best when you do. Do you think Tristram's awake?"

"You can look."

Dinadan stepped into the rough doorway, paused to let his eyes grow accustomed to the gloom, then spied a large bundle on the one bed. "Sir Tristram?"

Tristram rolled over and looked at Dinadan. There was no recognition in his eyes. "How did you know my name? For I speak it to no one."

"I met you up the road a few weeks ago. My name is Dinadan."

"I know no one of that name."

"Yes, I remember that. Well, we were only together for a short time, and then you got preoccupied fighting some knight named Lickamat or something."

Tristram sat up with energy. "Sir Lamorak! He is a villain! I should have killed him!"

"Didn't you?"

"No, his lady appeared and ordered him to stop. Then she cast some sort of spell, and then next I knew I was alone."

"Some other time, perhaps. Listen, Sir Tristram, I was wondering if you could answer a few questions. For instance, how did you ever come to love the Lady Iseult?"

Tristram raised his chin in the air and looked forlorn. "Of that I may not speak. I've taken a vow —"

"Yes, yes, I know all about that. It's just that it seems so odd. After all, didn't you kill her father's friend and champion, Sir Marhault? So how come she doesn't consider you a worm and spit at the ground where you walk?"

"Iseult could never so demean herself. Who can say where Eros will send his feathered shaft deep into the bosom of another helpless soul? More than this I cannot say."

Dinadan didn't believe this, but he saw that pressing Tristram more now would only make him more mulish, and so he changed tactics. "I quite understand, and I can't tell you how inspiring your vow is. That's why I'm here. I thought maybe you should have a travelling companion who would speak for you when necessary. That way you would never be tempted to break your vow. I'd be happy to ride with you."

Tristram hesitated, but after declaring his vow so firmly, he could hardly say no, and he agreed. For the next hour, Tristram strolled about and talked to Brother Eliot, while Dinadan packed up his brother's things and saddled his horse. At last they were ready, and Tristram made a lengthy farewell speech to the monk, who endured it with great patience. Then Tristram lifted his head high and turned to Dinadan, "Very well, let us be off. I shall continue my silent path of sorrow."

"Of course you will," Dinadan said soberly. Brother Eliot made a faint choking sound.

"But see to it that you tell no one my name," Tristram added.

"If anyone asks, I'll tell them you are Sir Stultus," Dinadan replied. Brother Eliot choked again and turned his face, but he was able to raise a hand in reply to Dinadan's parting wave.

Dinadan waited almost an hour before he tried again to get information from Tristram. It was harder than he had expected. It wasn't at all difficult to get Tristram to talk; it was just that any question that mentioned Iseult reminded him of his vow and made him hold his tongue for a few minutes. During one of these lulls, Dinadan took out his rebec and began to play.

"That's a rebec!" Tristram announced. Dinadan didn't reply, having nothing to add to Tristram's information. Tristram continued, though. "I used to play the rebec a little, when I was small, but now I play the lyre."

His interest stirred, Dinadan stopped playing. "Do you?"

"Oh yes, I find it very useful in wooing ladies. You just tell them that you've written a song for them, and they fall all over you."

"Really?" Dinadan replied, cautiously. "Tell me how that works."

"It's very simple, really. That was how I wooed Iseult."

"I see," Dinadan said, carefully. "And it worked?"

"Until she got married," Tristram said mournfully.

"Married?"

"Yes, and King Mark watches his wife like a hawk."

"What?" Dinadan exclaimed, in consternation.

"Iseult is married to King Mark?"

"Didn't you know?"

"But how could that be? Isn't King Mark her father's worst enemy? Are you sure?"

But he had gone too far. Tristram raised his chin in a noble pose. "My lips are sealed," he said grandly.

And sealed they stayed, at least on the subject of Iseult and King Mark. After two more frustrating hours, they arrived at a small inn, built at a crossroads in the forest. Dinadan was pleased to see it, since he generally had a good relationship with innkeepers, but the keeper of this inn did not seem at all pleased. As soon as they rode into sight, the innkeeper rushed out of the front door waving his arms frantically at them. "Oh no, oh no. Not two more! Go away, I tell you! We're tired of knights, and the stories are all lies anyway! Go away!"

Dinadan stared in consternation, but Tristram replied sharply, "I turn aside my path for no man, let alone for a villein such as thee."

The innkeeper's face sagged wearily. "But I tell you, it's all lies. I never made such a rule, and I never will. Why would I do such a thing anyway?"

"What are you talking about, friend?" Dinadan asked gently. "What rule? We mean you no harm."

"The rule about fighting a joust before.... Do you mean you haven't heard about —?"

"Is this indeed the Inn of Challenge?" Tristram asked eagerly. "I had heard of it, but did not know it was here!"

"No, I tell you! It's all a lie. This is the Green Dragon Inn. All that stuff about —"

"Then this is the inn where no knight is permitted to lodge save he joust first! A noble place."

Dinadan looked sympathetically at the innkeeper. "Is that what people say about your inn?" The keeper nodded glumly. "Sounds like it would be bad for business. Why don't we just ride on?"

The innkeeper's eyes brightened, but Tristram would have none of it. "Fie, for shame! Bring out your knight, and we shall assay him by dint of weapons."

"Dent of brain, you mean," Dinadan muttered. "Look here, ah, Sir Stultus, maybe this fellow doesn't have a knight handy. Surely we aren't expected to wait around until one happens along."

The innkeeper looked more weary than ever. "Why not? That's what those other chaps are doing." And then, as if on cue, two knights strolled out of the inn and caught sight of Tristram and Dinadan. The larger of the two, who was the only one in armour, let out a cry of triumph and ran to his horse.

"Come, friend!" Tristram shouted. "Let us

have ado with those two knights!"

"No, thank you," Dinadan said. He turned to the innkeeper. "Sorry about this. I didn't know."

"Not your fault," the man replied. "I'll get a spade to bury the loser with the others."

Dinadan walked his horse up to the inn, where the second knight still stood, watching. He was a tall, angular man with sandy hair and a serious face, but he smiled pleasantly at Dinadan. "Not joining your companion in the challenge?" the strange knight asked.

"I was just going to ask you the same thing," Dinadan replied. "But since you ask: no."

They stood together at the door of the inn and watched while Tristram and the large knight made their preparations for combat. "This knight in the pretty gold armour, is he a friend of yours?" the strange knight ventured.

"Not really. Just riding together."

"Ah, that's the same with me and Sir Lamorak, there."

Dinadan looked up sharply. "Sir Lamorak! For heaven's sake, don't say that name to my companion! He's sworn to kill Lamorak."

"Why? What's your companion's name?"

"Sir... Sir Stultus."

The stranger's serious face softened. "Ah. A

Latin fellow, I gather."

"You speak Latin?"

"I know what *stultus* means, anyway."

Dinadan suppressed a smile. "Well, it's more of a description than a name, really. He's keeping his real name secret."

"Ah, it's Tristram, then. I'd heard he was about." The knight grinned at Dinadan. "My name's Gaheris, of King Arthur's table."

Dinadan smiled in reply. "My name's Dinadan, and I'm from Arthur's table, too, even though I've only been there once. You must have been away then."

Gaheris smiled broadly. "I was, but I've heard of you. You went off with Kai and Bedivere and that young fellow who wants to be a knight, didn't you?" Dinadan nodded. "How's that business going?" Gaheris asked. Dinadan rolled his eyes and told Gaheris about King Isbaddadon's tasks. Gaheris shook his head sadly. "I imagine Kai's about to kill someone," he commented. "So what's your lad – What's his name? Culloch? – doing now?"

"He's supposed to be finding some magic picnic basket or other."

"The Magic Picnic Basket of Guidno?" Gaheris asked.

"You've heard of it?" Dinadan asked, astonished.

"Ay. Guidno's shop is just over the hill in the next

town. He's a caner – chairs, baskets, and the like. Poor fellow thought it would be good business to spread a story about how his baskets were so big that they'd never be empty, and the tale got out of hand. His shop's been broken into about once a week since the story began by people wanting the eternal picnic."

"So it's all a lie?"

"An exaggeration. But either way, it's come back to haunt the teller."

Dinadan took a breath, his mind racing. "So... so he wouldn't mind if the story got told around how the great Culloch captured his magic basket and took it to King Isbaddadon? I mean, people would leave him alone then, wouldn't they?"

Gaheris's eyes lit up with inner laughter. "You've a good head on you, Dinadan. I'll help you. Let's go talk to Guidno."

Dinadan jerked his head at Tristram and Lamorak, who had managed to unhorse each other and were sparring heavily with their broadswords. "What about them? Hate to leave them to kill each other."

"We could toss some water on them."

"They'll just rust. Here, let me try this." Dinadan strolled over to the combat. "Sir knights! You do yourselves great dishonour! For how shall you win the Tournament of Women if you slay each other here?"

The two knights lowered their swords, gasping. "What tournament is that?" Tristram asked.

"Have you not heard? The Tournament of Women begins at this same hour two days hence in... in York. If you are to win the prize there, you must leave at once!"

It worked. The knights separated, swearing that they should meet again in the tournament, at which time they would surely teach each other a lesson, and within ten minutes they were gone, taking separate paths. Gaheris watched them go, then turned to Dinadan. "A very great pleasure it is meeting you, Sir Dinadan. A knight after my own heart you are."

Dinadan was pleased, but then his face clouded. "A knight who hates to fight and who tells lies? Are you sure?"

Gaheris's face grew serious. "Would you rather be like them? Two mighty warriors racing each other to an imaginary tournament to win a prize that only exists in their own minds?" He shrugged. "Let's go and talk to Guidno."

A week later, having regretfully said goodbye to Gaheris and having even more regretfully rejoined

Culloch and the others, Dinadan rode back into King Isbaddadon's castle to deliver the basket that Guidno had willingly given him. In return, Dinadan had wasted no opportunity in the last week to tell a fanciful tale he had concocted about how Culloch had fought a great ogre for the hamper.

As it turned out, Dinadan's tale arrived at King Isbaddadon's castle before Culloch and his company did, and the king welcomed them back with open arms, proclaiming that they would feast together that very night. He barely gave the basket a glance, which was just as well, as a more ordinary basket would be hard to produce, but he embraced Culloch like a long-lost son. He had evidently forgotten his initial dislike of his daughter's suitor.

The feast proceeded along the same lines as his earlier feasts, with more food and drink than even Culloch could polish off, but Dinadan ate little. He had to be awake at midnight to visit the kitchens. Twice during the feast, Dinadan was able to catch the eye of Lady Brangienne, who was standing at her usual place behind Lady Olwen. Neither gave any signal, but Dinadan was confident that Brangienne would meet him later.

He was not disappointed. Just after midnight, as Dinadan was finishing an excellent plum pudding, she appeared. "I hope you've left something for me," she commented, eyeing the empty platter.

"Some roast boar in the larder," Dinadan said. "How have things been here?"

Brangienne made a face as she filled a plate. "Need you ask? Olwen grows daily more repulsive. All she talks about these days is her gallant lover."

"Culloch?" Dinadan asked. Brangienne nodded and Dinadan rolled his eyes. "That *is* repulsive. She doesn't really think he does all this business out of love for her, does she?"

"She might; she's stupid enough. But even if she knows he's just playing a silly game with her father, she can't very well say so. Think how it would make her look." Brangienne rolled her eyes and tossed her hair out of her face. "Love!" she said, with loathing.

Dinadan seized the opportunity. "Doesn't make sense, does it? For instance, why would Iseult fall in love with Tristram, who killed her father's best friend? For that matter, why would she marry King Mark, the one who sent Tristram to do the deed?"

Brangienne's eyes grew wary, and she chewed in silence for a long moment. At last she said, "You've been busy, haven't you?"

"Only my ears," Dinadan said quietly. "My tongue has been still. I've told no one where you are."

Brangienne was silent for another minute. Then she looked seriously into Dinadan's eyes. "It's the price of my life if the story gets out. I should tell no one." Her eyes narrowed. "Why do you care?"

Dinadan shrugged. "I don't know," he replied truthfully. "Maybe I could help."

Brangienne frowned again, then took a breath. "Unlikely. But for what it's worth, I suppose I trust you to keep silent, and it would be a relief to tell someone. Make yourself comfortable." Then she began. "I've told you how King Mark challenged King Aguissance and how their two champions, Tristram and Marhault, fought and how Tristram killed Marhault." Dinadan nodded, and Brangienne said, "Well, something else happened at that tournament: King Mark saw Iseult. I've told you how beautiful she is. Mark must have made up his mind right away that he had to have her for his wife."

"After defying her father and killing his friend? Rather a tall order."

"You would think. But about six months later, a strange minstrel arrived at our gate, a beautiful man with broad shoulders."

"A minstrel, hey?" Dinadan asked, interested. "Any good?"

Brangienne almost smiled. "Not as good as you

are, if that's what you're wondering. Only played the lyre, which can get very tiresome. His name, he said, was Tramtris."

Dinadan closed his eyes and nodded with comprehension. "Tramtris," he repeated. "That was the best he could come up with. Didn't you recognise Tristram?"

"We'd never seen him except in full armour. He came, he said, as an emissary from a great and distant king who had heard of Iseult's beauty and wished to marry her."

"King Mark, of course," Dinadan said. "But he wouldn't tell you the king's name, I'll wager."

"He said the king had taken some sort of vow." Dinadan sighed and nodded again. Brangienne continued. "King Aguissance said no, at first, but Tramtris came with a great retinue and handed out so much gold that Iseult was fascinated by her mystery suitor. In the end, she convinced her father to let her go." Brangienne took a breath. "And as her chief lady-in-waiting, I went, too. Before the king sent us away, though, he called me aside and gave me something."

Brangienne grew silent, staring moodily into a cold fireplace. Dinadan waited as long as he could, then asked, "What was it?"

"A love potion, bought at great price from a

sorceress. You see, Aguissance was afraid that Iseult would be disappointed with the mysterious king, and he wanted her to be happy. So he bought this potion. I was to pour it in her drink on her wedding night. It would make her fall forever in love with the first person her eyes saw after she drank it."

"Scary stuff," Dinadan commented. "Did it work?"

Brangienne shook her head. "Not the way it was supposed to. On the ship to Cornwall, I left the flask in my cabin one day. When I came back, I found Iseult and Tristram in my room, drinking from the flask and looking into each other's eyes."

"I see," Dinadan said. "But... but what were they doing in your room going through your things?"

"Does it matter?" Brangienne asked. "The damage was done. They were in love, and I suppose will be until they both die. It was my fault."

Dinadan frowned. It didn't seem to him that Brangienne had done anything wrong, but he wasn't going to argue. "Must have been quite a scene when you got to Tintagel," he said. "Iseult finding out that her mystery betrothed was King Mark, and King Mark finding out that his future queen was in love with Tristram."

Brangienne shuddered. "I don't want to think about that day. But, one thing: Mark never found out about the potion. Iseult and Tristram are the only ones who know."

"Except for you... oh!" Understanding came in a flash. "That's why you ran away. You're a threat."

Brangienne looked speculatively at Dinadan. "I have to admit that you have more wit than the average man. You're right. One night, just after the wedding, I overheard them talking, and I distinctly heard Iseult tell Tristram that I was dangerous. I left the court that hour. They found me, though."

"The guards in the forest," Dinadan said. "And you think that they're still looking for you? To conceal their secret?"

"You have to know King Mark. He's a madman. If he finds out, he'll kill Iseult. As long as I'm alive, I'm dangerous to her."

"What a tale," Dinadan said, musing.

"A tale you'll never tell!" Brangienne said fiercely.

"I didn't say it was a good tale," Dinadan said. "A good tragedy should be about grand emotions and great deeds that go awry, not about two fools drinking from the wrong flask. No, I won't be tempted to tell this one at all." He looked up at Brangienne. "But you may be sure that if I can ever help, I will."

Brangienne nodded, then turned and left without speaking. She did not look to Dinadan to be very reassured.

6

THE SHADOW

OF THE WOODS

"Gather round, now, Culloch lad! Hear your next trial!" King Isbaddadon bellowed. He was standing before the assembled knights in his courtyard, shortly after dawn, and his face showed a mixture of triumph and discomfort. The discomfort probably came from a headache, Dinadan reflected: anyone who had caroused as late as the king had the preceding evening would feel out of sorts at this hour. But the look of triumph came from what he had to say. The king shouted again. "This task will be harder than all the others."

"You might think it so, but for me it will be easy," answered Culloch. The bravado of his reply

117

was spoiled by a faint moan at the end. He had caroused as hard as the king.

Bedivere leaned forward to hear the task, perhaps hoping for a worthy task, but Dinadan only sighed resignedly. He saw nothing in King Isbaddadon's leering grin to inspire hope.

"Your next task," the king announced importantly, "is to bring to the Lady Olwen a comb made from the bristles of the great boar Torch Troyth, who lives in the woods near Caernarvon!"

Bedivere winced. "My lord, this is ridiculous. These are not tasks but market errands. I beg you —"

"I am not finished!" the king roared. "This boar must be hunted with the famous Hound of Druddwyn, and the hound must be held with a leash woven from the great beard of Dillus the Bearded."

"The man's daft," Sir Kai grumbled.

"And finally," Isbaddadon said, "the hunt must be led by Mabon, son of Modron, who was stolen away from his parents when he was barely three days old!"

"What?" asked Bedivere.

"Eh?" Sir Kai said.

The king crowed delightedly. "That's right! Modron is a merchant, and his oldest son was stolen from his cradle fifteen years ago, and he has never been seen again! Do you still think that you will find the task easy, my boy?" He uttered a sharp crack of laughter, but stopped immediately and began gently to rub his temple.

A slow smile grew on Bedivere's face. "At last," he said.

"Ay, finally a real task," Sir Kai said. "For all the good it'll do us. You don't really think we can find a lad missing fifteen years, do you?"

"I'd rather fail at an impossible task that's worth trying than succeed in every pointless chore under the sun," Bedivere replied. "Come on, Culloch. Let's go."

Culloch wanted to begin by looking for Dillus the Bearded, so that he could make his leash, but the other three overruled him, and they went immediately to look for Modron the merchant to find out everything they could. His shop was not far from Isbaddadon's castle, and within an hour they were standing before the stout, black-bearded tradesman. He smiled ingratiatingly at them, "My lords! My lords! You do me great honour! Please come in! Woman! Fetch wine for our distinguished guests! You, boy! Bring out the brocade!"

"We need no wine, friend," Bedivere said.

"I'll have some," Culloch interjected. "Have you

anything to eat with it?"

"But of course, my lord. Please sit down." He looked angrily about until he spied a small, pudgy girl. "Girl! You! What are you doing just looking at us! Go fetch a chair for his worship! Four chairs!" Modron looked back at the knights, and his face beamed with benevolence and hospitality. "I can see that you have heard of my latest shipment of brocade, perfect for your ladies' gowns. Really, though, I am not sure that I intend to sell it. It was so costly, and I really meant it for my own dear wife. But since you have come so far —"

"You are mistaken, sir," Bedivere replied gently. "We have not come to buy brocade."

"Ah, but wait until you see it," the merchant added eagerly. "To see it is to want it, I assure you! Boy! Where's that worthless scrub! I said, bring out the brocade!"

The boy who had been sent for the cloth reappeared, struggling with a long bolt of shimmering material. He bumped against a table and a pottery tankard fell to the floor and cracked. The merchant exploded with oaths, and the boy – evidently acting on past experience – simply dropped the cloth on the floor and ran. The merchant screamed threats after him until Bedivere took him by the shoulder and physically turned him around.

"Stop, sir, I beg you," Bedivere said sternly. "It was not the lad's fault. I told you, we are not here to buy cloth. Leave your servant alone."

This stopped Modron. "Servant? My lord, I have no servants. I am a poor man. That was my son, worthless dunderhead though he is. But come, will you not look at the brocade?"

"Your son?" Bedivere repeated, frowning. "Your second son, I take it?"

"Nay, that one is fourth – or maybe fifth – of my sons, and each as ungrateful as the last."

Bedivere frowned, but he pressed on. "Actually, it is regarding one of your sons that we have come. We were told that your eldest son, one Mabon, was stolen from you, and we are pledged to find him."

"Oh, ay, the ungrateful wench!" the merchant said, scowling furiously.

"Wench?" Sir Kai asked. "What wench?"

"Nothing, nothing, your worship," the merchant replied hastily. "Yes, my oldest was stolen from me by witches or whatnot, when he was barely born. Probably dead by now."

"Why would you say that?" asked Bedivere.

"Sickly brat, like his mother, curse her."

Bedivere's face grew even more severe, and he started to speak, but at that moment a pale, stooped woman appeared, carrying four cups of wine. Culloch said, "At last!" and took the whole tray from her with one hand. Bedivere ignored the wine and asked through tight lips, "Could you tell us about the night he was taken? Do you know which direction the thieves went?"

While the men talked, the woman who had brought the wine crept away to the other side of the store and got down by a bucket of water and began to scrub the floor. Pretending to look at the merchandise spread out on tables, Dinadan left the others and strolled over beside her. She glanced up once, furtively, and Dinadan saw to his surprise that she was not as old as he had thought. She could not have been much more than twenty-five years old, too young to have been the stolen baby's mother. But, thought Dinadan, the tradesman had just said he had no servants.

"I beg your pardon, my lady," Dinadan said in a low voice. The woman looked up fearfully. "I am sorry to disturb you, but perhaps you could help me."

The woman's eyes flickered toward the merchant, then returned to Dinadan. "Yes, your worship?" she whispered.

Dinadan knelt beside her, behind a large barrel of flour. "We are here to look for that fellow's missing son Mabon. Are you… are you Modron's daughter?"

"His wife, your worship," the woman whispered. Dinadan stared at her, pity and puzzlement on his face. "His third wife," the woman explained. "His first two wives, God help them, are dead."

Dinadan bit back a trenchant comment on the previous wives' good fortune and said only, "And the missing boy, Mabon?"

"He was the first wife's. They *say* she died right after the boy was took."

Dinadan caught the woman's inflection. "What do you mean, 'they *say*'? Do you doubt it?"

The woman looked again at her husband, and her eyes were bright with hatred. "I never seen her grave, nor nobody hereabouts has. If she died like he said, where'd he lay her, then?"

Dinadan was not sure what she was implying. "Do you think he killed her? Or that she ran away? Then by all the gods, why did you take her place? Why did you marry that creature?"

The woman's face hardened, and she said very softly, "I was alone in the world. My parents were old and poor, and when they died I had nothing. I am not a pretty woman, and he is a rich man. How else was I to keep myself warm and fed? And now there are the children."

"Your children? Those two little ones?"

The woman nodded. "They're all he has left now.

All his older children ran off as soon as they was old enough, but does he think about that when he pulls out his belt to beat them? No." She returned to her scrubbing with fury, as if the floor were her enemy. Dinadan watched her for a moment, a sense of helpless anger filling his breast.

"Will your husband beat the boy for breaking that cup?" he asked suddenly. The woman looked up, her eyes glinting with tears, and she nodded curtly. Dinadan reached into the pouch at his belt and drew out two golden coins. "I cannot change your husband, my lady. He is as he has made himself. But give these to your son and tell him that Sir Dinadan sends his regards."

The woman's eyes widened, and she quickly secreted the coins in the folds of her dress. "Thank you, your worship," she said faintly. "And sir? I remember hearing that his first wife came from the east and had people there. Near Chester. Her name was Rhiannon, same as mine. You should look there."

Dinadan nodded silently, rose, and walked back to where the others stood. Culloch was finishing off the third cup of wine while Bedivere and Sir Kai still talked with the merchant. For his part, Modron seemed to have realised that these knights were not going to buy anything, and he was growing each moment more recalcitrant. Dinadan stooped and picked up the cracked mug from the floor, where it still lay. "What do you want for this, my man?" he asked abruptly.

"For that?" Modron asked, bewildered. "But it's —"

Dinadan flipped a silver coin to him. "Is that enough?" The merchant nodded, for a moment speechless, and Dinadan turned to the others, "Come on. We're wasting time here." Then he turned on his heel and walked out, followed by the others. Culloch came last. Dinadan carefully put the cup in his pack, then pointed his horse east toward Chester.

After a few minutes, Sir Kai rode up beside him. "You paid that worm twenty times what that cup was worth, even if it wasn't cracked," Sir Kai commented. It was not a question.

Dinadan shrugged. "And for all that, it wasn't half what that little boy will pay."

Sir Kai nodded. "Likely." He smiled suddenly. "And you thought that maybe since you paid for the cup, Modron wouldn't beat the boy so hard." Sir Kai chuckled.

"Maybe." Dinadan changed the subject. "We're going to Chester, Sir Kai. That's where the boy Mabon's mother was from. Her name was Rhiannon. Maybe we can find someone there who can help us."

They rode together wordlessly for a few seconds. "You can drop the title, lad. Just call me Kai," the great knight said suddenly. Then they were silent again.

They camped that night in a clearing in the woods. Dinadan lay down after dinner, feeling exhausted, but sleep did not come to him. After he had been lying awake for almost an hour, the moon rose over the edge of the trees and washed the clearing with its pale light – not bright enough to make the world lighter, only enough to make the shadows blacker. Dinadan sat up, his mind returning to Rhiannon and her children back at the shop, and he knew he would not sleep this night. Taking up his rebec, he slipped into the woods and walked a furlong into the shadows, where he would not disturb his companions' rest.

Dinadan began to play. He did not sing; there were no words for the song that he felt this time. He played slow, mournful notes, making up the tune as he went along, hardly caring which note followed which, so long as each note was played in purity, with as rich a tone as his hand and instrument could produce. He tried to form each note into the shape of an unloved wife's grief, the sort of grief that has no end in sight before death, no revenge but the private revenge of secret hatred.

There was a rustling at his feet, and Dinadan looked down to see two rabbits, ears cocked, sitting not two feet away, listening. He nodded absently at them but continued playing. In a moment, there was another motion, and Dinadan saw the large unblinking eyes of a deer behind a nearby deadfall. He paused and looked up. The deer retreated into the darkness, the rabbits hopped away, and a faint rustling came from every side. He looked about but saw nothing.

Taking up his rebec again, he resumed his song, and within seconds the rabbits and the deer had returned, along with a fox, a badger, several hedgehogs, and a sleek otter. Birds alighted in the branches above his head, without any sound but the faintest ruffling of wings. The air was thick, and Dinadan felt light-headed, but he continued his song, now playing not only for Rhiannon but also for his woodland audience.

More animals appeared, and then, from behind Dinadan came a gentle piping sound, like the wind whistling through chinks in a wall, but the piping kept time with Dinadan's song. Slowly, the piping grew clearer and closer, and then, to Dinadan's wonder, began to play in counterpoint to his own melody. Amazed, but too full of music to be

127

afraid, Dinadan continued playing, picking up the tempo and playing furiously, playing – as he realised later – beyond his own ability. The piping kept time, joining the melody for brief moments, then branching away in wild harmonies. More animals gathered. Dinadan was dimly aware that a great brown bear had joined the crowd, sitting on the forest floor with rabbits and squirrels gathered fearlessly around its heavy paws.

Dinadan did not know how long he played, but at last there came a time when he knew the song was ending, and he slowed down to play the last refrain. The piping slowed with him and ended at the same moment, and then there was silence. This time the animals did not retreat, and Dinadan wondered briefly if he ought to be afraid, but he hardly cared. "Who are you?" he said softly, not turning around.

"I am Sylvanus," answered a clear, musical voice. "And I am your servant, dear Dinadan."

"You know me?" Dinadan asked.

"Not until this moment," the voice replied, "but now I know you as well as you know yourself. You called me with your music. Few mortals are given such magic."

Dinadan swallowed. "Then you… are not a mortal?"

"No." A shadow moved at the corner of his eye and Dinadan turned his head to see the outline of a small horned figure, human in shape except for goat-like legs. The animals had all turned their attention away from Dinadan and were watching this shape, this Sylvanus. "Tell me," the little figure asked. "Did you play from your own grief or of the grief of another."

"I was thinking of… of a woman I met, who is married to a beast."

"It is very strange," Sylvanus said conversationally, "but it always seems to me that the sort of men that are called 'beasts' are not very beastly at all, but are rather the most human."

Dinadan smiled slowly, then turned to the assembled animals. "You are right. I beg your pardon, all of you. I shall be more careful in the future how I speak of you."

"Oh, I wasn't complaining," Sylvanus said mildly. "After all, when bear cubs misbehave, their mothers call them 'boys' or 'girls'. Is that not so, ma'am?" The brown bear nodded slowly in reply.

"She understood you? You speak to the animals?" Dinadan asked, amazed.

"Of course," Sylvanus replied. "Is there something you wished to ask them?"

"Oh, no. I was just surprised."

"Are you sure? Have you no questions?"

Dinadan stopped, thinking. Sylvanus appeared to be prompting him. "No, nothing. Unless... unless they could tell me about a small baby – a human baby, I mean – that was stolen about fifteen years ago and may have been carried through these woods."

Sylvanus hesitated. "That will be difficult. Few of these creatures gathered here were alive then, and even among those who were, the notion of keeping count of years would be foreign. But my lady bruin here may know something."

Dinadan heard no words, not even any sounds, pass between the shadow and the bear, but the bear's countenance grew very intent and her eyes stayed fixed on Sylvanus's form. After several minutes, the shadow spoke. "I do not know if this will help or not. She says that there has been no stolen baby in these woods as long as she has lived, which I judge to be at least twenty years. She does remember, though, that many years ago a young woman, hardly old enough to be a mother, brought her baby through here. Was the child a boy?"

"Yes," Dinadan replied, suddenly convinced he had his answer. This was Modron's first wife. No wonder the merchant had spoken of her so harshly. She had run away with her child.

"She says that the woman had just borne the

child and was very weak, too weak to be travelling alone, but she came this way, travelling only at night for two nights."

"Where did she go?"

"That is hard to explain. The landmarks that the wood creatures know are not the ones that you would recognise, or even see, since they are as much about smells and feelings as they are about sight. Wait a moment."

There was another long silence, and then a fox stepped forward, placed one paw on Dinadan's knee and looked deeply into his eyes.

"Tomorrow," Sylvanus said, "follow Renard here. He will show you."

"Thank you," Dinadan said, with wonder, both to the shadow and to the fox. The fox nodded and then slipped noiselessly away. The other animals also began to scatter, and Dinadan looked up quickly at the outline of his friend. "Sylvanus?"

"Yes?" the piper's voice was faint.

"Will we play together again?"

"Surely," came the reply. "Surely." And then Sylvanus was gone, and Dinadan's heart was full as he walked slowly back to the camp.

The next morning, Dinadan said nothing to the others, but he made certain that he was the first one to break camp so that the others would have to follow him. He saw no fox, but he pushed ahead, and a few minutes after starting he was rewarded with a glimpse of a tawny hide in the underbrush. Without hesitation, Dinadan left the path and headed into the brush.

"Hey, Dinadan!" Bedivere called. "Where are you going?"

"Follow me!" Dinadan called back, though he was not at all sure that they would. If Culloch, for instance, had led them into these thickets, Dinadan would have promptly parted company with him and kept himself to the path. But Dinadan heard them crashing into the bushes behind him. "Quickly," he said to the fox, hoping that somehow it would understand. Dinadan didn't want the others to catch up and ask him questions that he had no intention of answering.

It was a rough ride, but the fox seemed to understand what Dinadan wanted. It went slowly enough that he never lost track of it, even as he had to crash heavily through thickets that the fox slipped through with ease. At the same time, though, it went fast enough that Bedivere and Kai and Culloch never quite caught up. Dinadan's skin was scratched and bleeding, and his clothes were torn, and he was just beginning to doubt he could go on much farther when the fox stopped in a hollow under an ancient elm tree and looked up at Dinadan.

Without being sure why, Dinadan knew that this was the place to which the fox had been leading him. He dismounted, and the fox walked over to him and placed one paw on Dinadan's leg, just as he had done the night before. "Thank you, Renard," Dinadan said in a whisper.

In a blink, the fox was gone. Dinadan stood beneath the great tree, alone but for the wind and the thick layer of leaves. Then he saw it, a human skull at the base of the tree trunk, worn and weather-stained, but definitely human. Dinadan had just stooped to examine it when the others arrived, their horses lathered and panting.

"About time you stopped," Culloch said, gasping with exertion. "What were you thinking, riding off into the bush like that, when there was a perfectly good path?"

"What do you have, lad?" Kai asked curtly. Dinadan gestured at the skull, and Kai dismounted and joined him. "Let's take a look," Kai said. He knelt and began digging in the loam at the tree's base. In a moment, he had unearthed another bone, then a strip of embroidered cloth, faded but still clearly an intricate piece of work. Wordlessly, Kai handed the material to Bedivere, who had dismounted beside them.

Bedivere examined it for a moment, then said, "A woman's dress, I would say, and not of the latest fashion. But then, that much is obvious."

They both looked at Dinadan, who had been sitting beside the skull, watching Kai dig. Kai spoke. "Can you tell us anything about this, lad?"

Dinadan hesitated, but he had no reason to lie. "Modron's first wife, I would say. Rhiannon the first. She ran away after her baby was born. Is the baby there, too, Kai?"

Kai shrugged. "I'll look. Give me a hand, Bedivere?" Bedivere nodded, and Kai looked at Dinadan.

He shook his head and glanced down at the skull. "I'll stay with her," he said.

Culloch, the only one still on horseback, snorted and said, "I don't see what you're on about. We're not looking for a woman after all, and besides, I still think we should have begun with Dillus the —"

"Shut up, Culloch," said Kai.

They found more bones and the rest of the woman's dress, but no sign of a baby. They wrapped the bones and the skull in the remnants of the dress, then buried them deep. Bedivere said a few quiet words over the grave, and then Dinadan took out his rebec. Quietly, he played a brief passage from the elegy he had played with Sylvanus. Even Culloch was quiet while he played, and the wind brought a faint piping sound from across the forest. Dinadan lowered the rebec, and they rode away. Nobody asked Dinadan any questions.

Not half a mile further, they came upon a small cottage in the woods. There was a neat garden plot, and a few chickens and cows in the yard. An elderly man and woman sat on a bench outside the cottage, enjoying the sun, and from the woods nearby came the sound of an axe.

"Good morning," Bedivere said to the old couple.

"Good morning, sirs," they stammered, bowing deeply. Clearly they were unused to visits from knights.

"Don't be afraid," Bedivere said kindly. "We mean no one any harm, and we are as surprised to see you as you to see us. Is this not a very secluded place to make your home?"

"Yes, your worship," the man replied, bowing again. "But Beatrice and me, we never needed more people than just ourselves."

"And Colin," the woman added. "Don't forget Colin." She turned to Bedivere and curtseyed awkwardly. "Our grandson," she explained. "He lives with us and takes care of us."

The sound of the axe stopped, and Dinadan saw a sturdy, black-haired youth step out from among the trees.

"Have you lived here long?" Bedivere asked.

"Almost twenty-five years now," the woman said. "It is a good life we lead."

"But how do you live? Do you have enough to eat?"

The woman took a quick breath. "Sakes! I've been out of the world so long that I've lost my manners. I haven't offered you a bite! Will you stay and eat with us? We have fresh venison and vegetables. Colin!"

"Here, grandmother," the youth said. "You stay there. I'll get the food."

Bedivere dismounted, and the others followed his lead. "I thank you, ma'am," he said. "In truth I would like to talk with you. You see, we are looking for someone whom we think passed this way."

"No one has passed this way in many weeks," the old man said.

"Let's eat first, then talk," Culloch said abruptly. "I'm hungry."

Dinadan tossed his reins to Kai. "I'll go and help the boy," he said and strolled after Colin. He found him in a small smokehouse behind the cottage, unhooking a haunch of venison. "Can I help?"

The boy looked Dinadan squarely in the eyes, and his gaze was direct and without guile. "Is that really what you want, sir?" The boy looked to be about fifteen years old.

"No. I wanted to speak to you alone," Dinadan replied simply.

"Why?" the boy's voice was firm, but polite. Very different from his father's voice, Dinadan reflected.

"We are here on a quest. We are looking for a baby that was lost, oh, about fifteen years ago. His mother stole him away from his father soon after the boy was born, and she took him through the woods near here. Sadly, though, she was not strong, and I believe that she died not far from this place."

The boy's gaze had not wavered from Dinadan's eyes. He did not speak.

"One of those knights out there," Dinadan continued, "is under oath to find the boy and take him on a boar hunt. Then, I imagine, the boy will be taken back to his father."

"Who is the boy's father?" Colin asked quietly.

"A rich merchant named Modron."

"Why did the boy's mother leave this Modron?"

"I would guess it is because the man's soul is made of shop goods and silver, and he cares for nothing else."

Colin was silent for a moment. Then he said,

"My grandparents are very old. Each month they are able to do less for themselves. Sometimes it is more than even I can do, keeping things going here." Dinadan nodded but didn't answer. Colin lifted his chin. "So, sir knight. What do you think happened to the baby?"

Dinadan smiled. "I see two possibilities. Either the baby was found and brought home by an elderly couple who lived nearby and who had no children of their own, or else he died in the forest by his mother. I think he died in the forest." Colin's eyes widened with hope, and Dinadan added, "The only problem is that we didn't find the baby's body. I was wondering if perhaps you had found it one time and buried it yourself."

Colin's face brightened with a joy more pure than any that a boy raised in the home of Modron the merchant would have ever known. "Yes," he said at once. "Now that you mention it, I did." Dinadan could not help returning Colin's smile, but Colin's face clouded again almost at once. "I must go and speak to my grandparents. You see, they sometimes tell a story about how many years ago, they found a baby left beside the forest path. There was no one else around, as if the baby had been left there by someone who... who then crawled back into the woods to die. It's all a silly tale, of course, but it would be best for them not to tell it today."

Dinadan nodded. "You go talk to your grandparents. I'll bring some food, and then I'll break the news to my companions."

Telling the others that Mabon, son of Modron, had died in the forest was a bit more ticklish than Dinadan had expected. Neither Bedivere nor Kai was a fool, and the appearance of a boy of about fifteen years of age so close to the body under the elm had already aroused their suspicions. With Colin's help, though, Dinadan was able at least to stop them from pursuing their suspicions. Culloch, of course, noticed nothing.

It was a lie, to be sure. There was no disguising that fact. At heart though was a greater truth: the son of Modron the merchant – the boy who would have been had he been raised in that household – was as dead as he could be. This young man, who had chosen a life of hard work and loneliness and duty to others over the life of a rich merchant's son, and had so chosen without even a second's hesitation, this was a different person entirely, a boy that Rhiannon the first would surely have been proud of.

Dinadan's mind turned now to the other Rhiannon and her two children, and a pleasing thought began to take shape. He waited until the knights had finished their meal, and then asked casually, "So where to now? Since Mabon's dead, the whole task is off."

Kai nodded judiciously. "Ay, that's true. Can't do any of it since this part's impossible."

"We could still hunt for Dillus the Bearded to make a leash," protested Culloch. "I always thought we ought to begin there any —"

"No, Culloch," Bedivere said. "The others are right. The only thing to do is to go back to King Isbaddadon and ask for another task."

Culloch brightened up perceptibly. "Oh, that would be all right. We could have another feast, and then he could send us out again. In fact, he'll probably just send us out on the same task, just leaving the boy out, don't you think?"

Bedivere's face grew stern. "If he does, Culloch, you'll go on that quest alone. I'll have no more to do with this foolishness."

"Hear, hear," Kai said, grinning. "I was wondering how long it would take you to come to that."

"But you've made a vow!" Culloch exclaimed.

"That I have. I vowed to stay with you until you were made knight or until you stopped trying to become one. To continue playing this child's game with Isbaddadon is to prove that you've no desire to be a true knight. If he gives you another silly chore, you shall have to decide whether you wish to stay with him or to go with me to seek knighthood."

Culloch looked both angry and confused, and Dinadan realised that Culloch had never seen any distinction between the great deeds demanded for knighthood at the Round Table and the tasks assigned by King Isbaddadon. Dinadan felt sorry for him, but there was no point in dwelling on Culloch's problem. He cleared his throat and said, "Say, lads. Someone ought to go tell that merchant fellow what's happened to his son."

"I didn't get the feeling he cared much," Kai pointed out.

"He ought to be told anyway," Dinadan said. "I'll do that while you three go back to Isbad's castle."

On the way back to Modron's shop, Dinadan hatched several plans for obtaining a private audience with Rhiannon the second, but as it turned out, they were unnecessary. When he arrived, Modron was gone, and Rhiannon and her two children were alone among the merchandise. Rhiannon's tired face relaxed as she recognised Dinadan. "Good morrow, your worship."

Dinadan bowed deeply and said, "I bring you good cheer, Mistress Rhiannon."

Rhiannon turned slightly pink at the courtly greeting. "Have you found the master's missing son?"

Dinadan ignored the question. "Mistress Rhiannon, did you not tell me that you cared for your aging parents until they died?" She nodded. "Was that very hard, madam?"

"It was hard, yes. But I loved them, you see."

Dinadan smiled. "Would it be too hard for you to do that again? I mean, could you and your children help care for an elderly couple on a small farm?"

Rhiannon's face fell. "I would like to, sir, if I could help. But I'm afraid my husband would never... there is so much work to do here."

Dinadan nodded sagely. "Yes, you're quite right. I shall have to take you all away from here, won't I? Do you need to pack anything?"

"Oh no, we own nothing here —" She broke off suddenly, and covered her face with her hands. "Oh, sir, you shouldn't say such things. My husband will never let us leave. After his last son ran away, he swore that he'd not let us out of his sight."

"Well, where is he now, then?"

"Only just across the square at the tavern. Please sir, don't give us hope. We can't leave. You'd only have to hear his vow to know how strong he felt. He swore he'd not let us leave till the day he opened up his shop and gave everything away for free."

Dinadan chuckled. "He said that, did he? Well, never mind. You three just come with me." Gently, but firmly, Dinadan led them outside to his horses. When he had Rhiannon and her daughter on his spare horse and the boy perched behind Dinadan's own saddle, he led both horses to the edge of town and then left them. "You stay here," he said to Rhiannon. "I won't be half a minute."

Drawing his sword, for effect more than for any other reason, Dinadan walked back across the village square to the busy tavern, where Modron sat alone at a table. "Modron!" Dinadan called. The hubbub of the tap room quieted, and Modron looked up. "Is it true," Dinadan asked, "that you swore a solemn oath that on the day that your wife and children got away from you you would open up your shop and give everything away for nothing?"

"What?" Modron demanded.

"Isn't that the oath you swore?" Dinadan repeated.

"Ay, that it is," interjected a man at a table nearby. "I heard it myself." A chorus of agreement rose from around the room.

"So what if it is?" Modron said. "What's it to you?"

"I just came to let everyone know: she's gone now." No one moved or spoke. Dinadan grinned at the townspeople. "Didn't you hear? Everything is free now. Go help yourselves." Then Dinadan turned on his heel and walked away. He had gone almost ten paces before the tavern doors flew open before the crowd racing across the square to the store, pushing aside the shrieking Modron as if he were a stray dog.

"What is all that noise?" Rhiannon asked nervously, when Dinadan reappeared.

Dinadan mounted and pointed the horses into the forest. "Nothing that concerns you anymore," he said.

7

THE MOOR & THE MORONS

Dinadan returned to King Arthur's great court at Camelot, where as months, then years, passed, he found himself becoming one of the best known and best liked of all the knights. It wasn't that he earned glory by feats of arms – only his friend Gaheris was more inept with sword and lance than Dinadan was – but he found himself nevertheless liked and even respected by nearly everyone he met. When he stopped to consider the matter, as he did occasionally, he could only guess that people holding parties and feasts liked to have someone to invite who would sing and tell tales without charging a minstrel's usual fee.

Dinadan's first years at court were eventful years for the Round Table. Sir Gawain, who had gone away on a quest that all had expected to end in his death, returned, telling a strange tale of facing a Green Knight and of earning honour through surrender. The great French knight Sir Lancelot, having been defeated in a tournament, renounced his knightly arms and rode away to live as a hermit. Gaheris went off on a quest, disappeared for a time, and then returned with a remarkable lady named Lynet on his arm and an even stranger tale to tell, far too strange to have been invented. And occasionally, word would come to court telling of events in the outside world. From Cornwall came several stories about Sir Tristram's secret love for Queen Iseult and of King Mark's madness as his suspicions grew. From Wales, there came other stories, of a young man who was hunting a boar with a magic hound or who was looking for something called the Magic Cauldron of Diornach. From this, Dinadan concluded that Culloch was still at it.

Culloch was alone now, though; Kai and Bedivere had left him after the quest for Modron the merchant's son. When King Isbaddadon had given Culloch another ridiculous task and Culloch had declared his intention to pursue it, then King Arthur's knights had written him off and departed. Judging from the reports, though, Isbaddadon was still finding odd jobs for his daughter's intended.

Dinadan rode out on quest himself a few times — mostly for form's sake — but he generally stayed away from Cornwall and Wales, not wanting to get involved again with either Tristram or Culloch. He did go to Cornwall once, to visit Brother Eliot at St Anselm's Abbey, and twice he went to Wales to see Colin and Rhiannon and the rest of the family in Sylvanus's Woods. It was a happy household there, and as one of the prime architects of that home, Dinadan took pleasure in its felicity. While in Wales, Dinadan had asked discreetly at a few inns, but he was never able to get any word of the Lady Brangienne. Not knowing how Brangienne was doing was the only drawback to avoiding Culloch, and Dinadan found himself thinking of her often.

About three years after leaving Culloch, while travelling through the Oxfordshire forest on a lazy and desultory quest – mostly riding cross-legged and playing the rebec – Dinadan caught the smell of roasting meat and heard the melodious strumming of an unfamiliar instrument. Following his senses, Dinadan guided his horses to a small clearing, where a large man sat by a fire. From the armour that was laid out neatly beneath a tree, Dinadan perceived that this was a knight, but he was like no knight he had ever seen. The armour was of an odd design, and most peculiar of all, the man's skin was as dark and brown as weathered wood. Dinadan stared. He had heard of the Moors – dark-skinned knights from Spain and Africa who fought well and bravely – but he had never seen one before.

The man rose to his feet at Dinadan's arrival. "I bid you good evening, O traveller." His voice was low and gentle, and his words, though clear, were pronounced in an unfamiliar manner. "As you see," the man continued, "I am taking of a fair repast soon. I would be honoured if you would share it with me."

In the dusk, the stranger's eyes seemed unnaturally large, perhaps because they were the only white spots on the man's face. Then the man smiled, showing gleaming teeth, and Dinadan grinned back. "I accept your hospitality, friend. My name is Dinadan."

The man bowed formally. "It is my honour, O my lord Dinadan. Your servant is named Palomides."

Dinadan dismounted and bowed back, feeling the need to match the Moor's formal politeness. "Forgive me for being inquisitive," Dinadan said, as he straightened up, "but did I also hear some music from your camp?"

Palomides bowed again, then produced a small, curious instrument, something like a child's longbow, strung with four strings. Palomides ran his fingers along these, producing a high-pitched but pleasing chord. "I was only playing to amuse myself in my solitude."

Dinadan produced his rebec. "I do the same thing," he said.

The Moor's formality melted visibly, and his smile grew broader. "This is indeed a fortunate meeting, my lord Dinadan. After you have eaten, perhaps we can share music."

The food was excellent, well-roasted and spiced with a delicious but unfamiliar seasoning that made Dinadan's mouth tingle. Eating took a long time, because his host would not eat until Dinadan had finished. Though Dinadan tried to get Palomides to join him, the Moor firmly declined, declaring that he really was not hungry, and that it was an honour to be able to give his food to Dinadan. When Dinadan had finished and had refused three times to eat more, then Palomides seemed to regain his appetite and was able to eat a healthy portion. Dinadan privately considered such politeness excessive, but he could not help feeling extraordinarily honoured by it.

When the Moor had eaten, Dinadan smiled and said, "And now, your music."

Palomides bowed his head and said, "My skill is small. I would much rather hear the music of my lord Dinadan, if you would permit."

Dinadan grinned. "Very well, friend. But only if you will promise to play for me when I have done." Palomides again protested that he had no talent, but his lips curled in a tiny smile, and Dinadan knew that he would hear from Palomides before he went to sleep that evening. "Here is a noble tale that I have heard told but have never sung." Dinadan took out his rebec and bow. "Perhaps you have heard of the good knight Sir Gawain?"

Dinadan proceeded to sing the tale of Sir Gawain's quest for the Green Knight. Dinadan was experimenting with some different techniques and had been working on this for some time. The tale went well, and although there were a few rough patches, Dinadan warmed to the story, allowing the rhythmic patterns of heroic songs to carry him along when he was unsure himself. As he came to the climax, where Gawain threw aside the charmed belt by which he had sought to save his life, the words flowed almost without check:

"'Behold,' cried Gawain, 'There my falsehood lies fallen!
Your cut taught me cowardice, care for my life,
I ever sought loyalty, love, and largesse,
But in falseness I find only fear.'

"Grasp once again, O Green Knight, your axe,
  And strike yet a second time after my shame.
  I will not resist, too wretched am I,
  And gladly I give myself here.'"

Dinadan finished the tale, telling how the Green Knight refused to take the life that was offered him, and how Gawain returned to court, made wise by failure. Dinadan played a final refrain on his rebec, then bowed his head, pleased and expecting applause. When none came, he looked up. Palomides was nodding gravely, his lips pursed.

"It is well that we have met," the Moor said at last. "For it is to know such things as this that I have come to this land."

Dinadan cocked his head and asked, "Such things as what?"

"The ways of knighthood." Palomides paused. "I am myself a knight, though the word is not used in my homeland. I fought against many of your knights at Jerusalem, and I found them to be worthy men of great courage. I came here to learn the secrets of their glory, for it seemed to me that a man can only grow stronger by learning of the strengths of others. I would like to meet this great man, Gawain."

Dinadan nodded. "He's just as great as I've told, even though he doesn't really talk like that. But you promised that I would hear you sing as well. What do you call that instrument?"

Palomides smiled modestly and said, "It has no name, for it is a trifle that I made myself and is like no other that I know. But my lord Dinadan has sung so well, I am ashamed to follow him. You must not ask me."

Interpreting this to mean that he should ask Palomides to sing at once, Dinadan did so. After another polite refusal, Palomides allowed himself to be persuaded. Taking up his instrument, he played a slow, quavering melody and then began to sing softly, in a different language. Dinadan leaned forward as he listened, and though he understood none of the words, he felt fascinated by the strange rhythms and curious chords. When Palomides stopped and put away his instrument, Dinadan asked, "What did your words mean?"

Palomides frowned with thought. "It is hard for me to put it into your language, for the words are made to echo each other in sound and meaning both. But it is a poem, by one of my homeland's greatest poets, called 'Sand of Life'. It says that all time is as sand, blowing in the desert, forming patterns and waves, but then changing with each new wind. It says that we living things are but small earthen vessels, formed for a time from grains of the sand of life, then shattered and driven back into the winds as particles that shape nothing for no purpose."

Dinadan nodded slowly. "Oh," he said.

"It is a poem much admired in the palaces and libraries of my country."

"A real crowd-pleaser, eh?" Dinadan said, still nodding. "I've never heard a song like it."

Palomides bowed. "You are too kind."

Dinadan bowed back. "Oh, no," he murmured politely.

Dreary poetry aside, Dinadan liked Palomides, and the Moor seemed to reciprocate. The next morning, by unspoken consent, they rode away together. Palomides wanted to meet the greatest knights of England, and Dinadan didn't have any objection, so they joined company. Palomides asked Dinadan many questions about the knights of the Round Table. He was disappointed to hear that Sir Lancelot, of whom he had heard even in distant lands, had left the court, but he hoped to meet other knights and learn from them. So it was that Palomides was delighted when after an hour or so they heard the unmistakable sound of sword on armour. Somewhere ahead at least two knights were fighting. "Come, Lord Dinadan, let us see what is before us."

Dinadan couldn't refuse, but it was with much less enthusiasm that he spurred his horse forward, and what little interest he had melted away at once when he came upon the battlefield. There fought two knights, and one of them wore shiny golden armour. "Oh, blast it," Dinadan muttered.

"What is it?" Palomides asked.

"Nothing. It's just that I think I know one of those knights, the chap in the gold."

"Is he an enemy of yours?" asked Palomides seriously.

"An enemy? Oh, no, I don't have any enemies," Dinadan replied.

Palomides's eyebrows shot up, and he stared at Dinadan with amazement. "None?"

"No, I don't think so. Well, there's one shopkeeper in Wales, but other than that, no. Tristram there isn't an enemy; just an annoyance."

"Tristram? Sir Tristram de Liones?" Palomides asked excitedly. "But I have heard of him! Surely he is one of the greatest knights living."

"He's very good with a sword, I believe," Dinadan replied guardedly. "But then, you can see that for yourself."

It was true. The battle that waged across the meadow before them was an impressive display of knightly prowess, on the part of both knights. It could have been quite enjoyable to watch from a technical standpoint, if it were not clear that the fight was in deadly earnest. Tristram and his opponent struck with lethal intentions, and between blows shouted insults and threats at each other. Palomides frowned, and Dinadan sighed. "Ah," he said. "That must be Sir Lamorak. He and Tristram don't get on, you see."

"Is it normal for English knights to speak thus to worthy opponents?" Palomides asked distastefully. "Such language is better suited to fishwives than to knights."

Dinadan shrugged. "It's normal for these two. They've hated each other for years, and the only surprising thing is that one hasn't killed the other yet."

At that moment, Dinadan felt suddenly very sleepy, as if morning had turned to night in a second. He fought the drowsiness for a moment, but it seemed so much easier to bow his head and take a short nap in his saddle. A moment later – or at least what seemed a moment later – the sleepiness fell away, and his first thought was that it was very quiet. The fighting had stopped. He lifted his eyes to see Palomides shaking his head sleepily and Tristram lying alone on the meadow before them. "What happened?" Dinadan asked.

"I can hardly say," Palomides replied. "But just

before the sleep came upon us, I saw a woman at the edge of the field. I fear we have been enchanted."

A vague memory stirred. "Oh, yes. I remember Tristram saying once that Lamorak's love is a faery lady who sometimes rescues him from danger."

Tristram began to move on the ground, and Palomides rode up to his side and dismounted. "Sir Tristram, may I give you my aid?" he asked.

Tristram sat up and took off his helm. "Who told you my name?" he asked.

Palomides blinked. "Sir Dinadan here told me."

"Dinadan?" repeated Tristram. "I know no one by that name."

Palomides glanced back at Dinadan, puzzled. "It's all right," Dinadan said with a sigh. "I'm not offended." He turned to Tristram. "It's been a few years since we met. How've you been? Still pining for Iseult, I gather?"

Tristram's eyes widened. "How came you to know about my love? It's a secret!"

"Oh yes, a secret," Dinadan replied. "Known only to you and Iseult and every minstrel in England."

Tristram struggled to his feet and turned to Palomides. "You must tell no one, do you understand?"

"No, I do not," Palomides replied quietly. "Why do you keep your love for a woman secret?"

Tristram tightened his lips and lifted his chin. Dinadan guessed that they were about to hear all about his vow of silence, and to head it off, Dinadan explained. "She's already married to someone else."

Palomides frowned again. "If this is so, then you must forget her. She has pledged herself to another, and that pledge must be honoured by all. Is it not so?"

Tristram seemed taken aback. "But she is the only woman I shall ever love. If I cannot have her, then I shall have no one."

"Then have no one," Palomides said. He turned to Dinadan. "Do English knights not show respect to the marriage vows of others?"

Dinadan answered honestly. "Some of us do. Others don't."

Tristram ignored this last exchange. "But if I have no lady, then I am no knight, for what is a knight for but to do service to a fair lady?"

Palomides looked at Tristram with a sort of horrified curiosity. "This is what you say is the purpose of knighthood? To serve a woman. This and no more?"

"What more could a man want?"

Palomides's face showed even more amazement, and he started to speak, but Dinadan cleared his throat and, catching Palomides's eye, shook his head briskly. Palomides closed his mouth, and Dinadan urged his horse forward, past Sir Tristram. "Very pleasant to have seen you again, Sir Tristram," Dinadan said politely. "Best of luck to you in performing service to ladies and all that, but we really must be moving along."

Palomides followed, and when they were out of sight, Dinadan stopped and looked back at the Moor. "Sorry about that, but you see I know that fellow, and that's the only thing you're likely to get out of him, that and lot of other rot about love, about which he knows nothing."

"But does he speak truth? That knights live only to serve ladies?"

"Some say that, especially the French minstrels. And some knights believe it, too. I don't know where the notion came from, but it isn't from King Arthur."

"What says King Arthur?" Palomides asked.

Dinadan paused a moment, collecting his thoughts. "King Arthur commands his knights to help the helpless. I suppose some people might interpret that to mean women. I wouldn't, myself, but that may be where the idea came from. And, to be fair, I suppose doing things for love is better than doing them for oneself. At least it isn't selfish."

"But of course it is," Palomides said firmly.

"Any love that calls for another person to dishonour her marriage is entirely selfish. Let us hope that the next knight we meet is more honourable than this Sir Tristram."

Unfortunately, the next knight, or would-be knight, that they met was Culloch. They were at a small tavern that Dinadan visited often, where the keeper loved a good song and set a good table for those who would give him one. Dinadan had just sung the tale of how Sir Lancelot had won the castle of Joyous Garde and was sitting down to a fine roast capon with Palomides, when he heard a roar of mirth from the back of the taproom. "I *knew* I'd seen you before!"

Dinadan turned to see a portly knight with a scraggly blond beard lurching toward him. It took Dinadan several seconds before he recognised this bellowing ox as Culloch. Dinadan sighed, but when Culloch reached their table, he forced himself to smile. "Hello, Culloch. How've you been?"

"Ho ho! I knew it was you when I saw you sing! It's just that I've forgot your name."

"Dinadan."

Culloch shook his head. "No, no, that's not it. Just wait. It'll come to me."

Dinadan nodded. "Well, let me know when it does. So, what've you been up to? You're not still running and fetching for King Isbad, are you?"

"The Sword of Wyrnach!"

"Beg pardon?"

"The Sword of Wyrnach!" Culloch repeated. He leaned closer and added, as if telling a secret, "He's a giant, you know."

"Who?" Dinadan asked.

"Wyrnach! It's my next task. I'm to bring back the Sword of Wyrnach the Giant to cut the roast at the wedding feast." Culloch pulled up a chair and sat down. "It's not as good as the last one, but still good. The last task was to bring back a magic cauldron, but here's the trick. It had to be kept boiling the whole time I was bringing it! Burned up four different oxcarts getting it home!"

Dinadan sighed, then turned to Palomides. "Sir Palomides, this is an old travelling companion named Culloch. Culloch, this is Sir Palomides."

Culloch looked for the first time at Palomides. "Your skin is dark!" he announced. Palomides did not speak, but his eyes looked faintly weary.

"Sir Palomides is a Moor," Dinadan explained.

"Can't he do anything about it?" Culloch asked.

"I suppose not," Dinadan replied, biting back a sharp retort. He was not happy to see Culloch, but now that he had found him, he wanted to ask him a few questions, and it would not do to offend.

"All the other tasks going along all right, then?"

"Oh, yes! It's been bang-up, doing knightly deeds for old Izzie."

"Knightly deeds?" Palomides asked, suddenly interested. "Are you a knight?"

"Not yet, but I'm working on it," Culloch replied grandly. "A great king is sending me out on quests."

Dinadan cleared his throat. "I thought that you were doing these things to win the hand of the Lady Olwen."

"Well, that, too. But when I've completed all these tasks, everyone will have to admit that I've earned knighthood."

"What sort of tasks do you do to earn knighthood?" Palomides asked.

That's torn it, Dinadan thought. Sure enough, Culloch launched into an enthusiastic description of the various tasks he had performed for King Isbaddadon. Palomides's expression grew more and more incredulous, as tale after foolish tale unfolded before them. Culloch managed to eat two roast chickens and drink several tankards of ale while he talked, which made his tales almost as hard to understand as they were hard to believe. As the telling grew longer, Dinadan began to worry that he would have no chance to ask his questions before Culloch fell asleep, but the story finally ended, and Culloch leaned back in his chair, as if to receive applause. Palomides was speechless.

"So, how long has it been since you were at Isbaddadon's court?" Dinadan asked.

"Eh? Not long. Week or so, I guess."

"Everyone there all right?" Culloch shrugged and nodded, and Dinadan pressed on. "How about that lady-in-waiting of Olwen's that we brought with us the first time, Lady Brangienne? Is she still there?"

"Brangienne?" Culloch repeated, his brow furrowed. "I don't think there's anyone there by that name. And I know everyone there."

"Brangienne's gone?" Dinadan said slowly.

Suddenly Culloch burst into laughter. "Oh, you mean Bragwaine! Ho ho! Mistress Cold and Stiff, I call her."

"Her name's Brangienne," Dinadan said, irritated.

"Izzie always calls her Bragwaine. Oh yes, she's still there. Why?"

"Just curious," Dinadan said. "Is she doing well?"

But this Culloch was not able to answer, since he had never really considered the matter, and Dinadan had to be content with the knowledge that Brangienne was still alive in Wales.

It was not long after this that Culloch began to nod off, which gave Dinadan and Palomides a reason to take their leave and return to the room that the innkeeper had given them for the night. Palomides did not speak until their door was closed, but then he said, in a voice rich with loathing, "*That* was an English knight?"

"No," Dinadan replied at once. "Nor is he likely to be. He didn't tell the whole tale." Dinadan then proceeded to tell how two of Arthur's most honoured knights had gone with Culloch to help him toward knighthood but had eventually given up on him. "You see, Sir Kai and Sir Bedivere were as disgusted by Culloch's games as you are."

Palomides considered this for a moment, then said, "It seems that I must go to the court of your King Arthur to find true knighthood, for the knights I find out here are not at all what I was looking for."

"We'll start that way tomorrow," Dinadan promised.

The two knights took the shortest road to Camelot, skirting Cornwall. At about midafternoon, riding alongside a gentle river, they came upon a hawking party. A dozen courtiers in fine clothes and at least that many ladies-in-waiting sat upon bored-looking horses, chatting and very occasionally directing a liveried falconer to send up a falcon. At the very centre of the party was a golden-haired lady in an extravagant gown, and as Palomides and Dinadan drew near, Palomides whispered, "What loveliness!"

The hawking party noted their approach and grew silent, watching the two knights. All eyes were on Palomides's dark features. The golden-haired beauty rode forward a few steps and smiled as she said, "Welcome, travellerth. Or should I say, wandering knighth?" Dinadan stared. When she had spoken the woman's beautiful face had assumed an expression of almost infantile pettishness. Her lips pushed out in a pout, and her eyes opened wide in a disconcerting way. She appeared to be imitating a spoiled five-year-old, though Dinadan could not imagine why.

Palomides bowed and replied. "We are indeed knights, and at your service, O lady, for you have already done us service, by granting us sight of such beauty."

Dinadan glanced quickly at Palomides, wishing for once that the Moor were not so excessively polite. In Dinadan's experience, little good ever came from paying ladies excessive compliments. The lady's eyes opened even wider. "It is alwayth my dearetht joy to meet knighth in thearch of adventure. I have been aided by more than one great champion when I was in dithtreth. May I know your names?"

"I am called Palomides, a knight from far Araby."

"And I," Dinadan said, "am named Dinadan."

The lady glanced at them speculatively, and for a moment Dinadan caught a calculating look in her eye that ill fit her assumed character. "It mutht be God's will that you have come to me, both of you," she said at last. "Two thuch gweat knighth, widing up to help a damthel in dithtweth."

As her artificial lisp grew increasingly infantile, the lady's face grew even more pouty. Dinadan looked away, revolted, but Palomides said politely, "I have come to this land to learn knighthood, and one knight has told me that a knight should serve ladies."

Dinadan glanced up, alarmed. "Yes, but don't forget that the one who told you that was an ass."

"But you said yourself a knight should serve those in need," Palomides replied. "How may I help you, my lady?"

The lady simpered and blinked rapidly for a few seconds, as if she'd got a bit of soot in her eye, and then sighed. "It is the thame quetht I thend evewy knight on, ath I have done for yearth and yearth and yearth, but becauthe I wuv her tho much, I will not thuwwendew."

"Will not what?" Dinadan asked.

"Surrender," the lady enunciated, casting a sharp glance at Dinadan.

"It must be wonderful to have a second language," Dinadan said.

165

"What lady do you love so?" Palomides asked.

"My own beloved lady-in-waiting has been stolen away from me this three years," the lady continued, abruptly dropping her lisp. "I fear she may be dead, but I must know. Please, great knight of Araby, I beg you to find her for me. Her name is the Lady Brangienne."

Dinadan was struck dumb for a moment, as he realised that this conniving woman before him was none other than Iseult, and in his surprise, he did not think fast enough. Before he knew what was happening, Palomides had bowed and said, "But this is easy, my lady. The Lady Brangienne is in Wales, at the court of one King Isbadd – how do you say his name, Dinadan?"

Dinadan opened his mouth, then closed it again.

"Isbaddadon!" Palomides said. "You need fear for her no more, for she is alive and in service to the king's daughter there. Is that not what your friend Culloch said, Dinadan?"

Dinadan closed his eyes with anguish, his mind racing. If Iseult was still hunting for Brangienne, that could only mean that she still wished to silence her. And now she knew where to find her. Dinadan looked up. "Yes, that's right. Will you be sending a messenger to her now, my lady?"

"But of course," Iseult replied, her eyes bright.

"Then let me tell you how to get to King Isbaddadon's castle," Dinadan said.

It was sad to part from the Moor, whom Dinadan had grown to like very much, but he had no time to waste. He had to get to Brangienne before Iseult's messengers did. Those messengers would be slowed down by the misleading directions Dinadan had given, but he knew that they would not be delayed long. Once they got to Wales, almost anyone they asked would be able to show the way.

Dinadan rode hard, pushing his horses long, resting them only briefly. He stopped nowhere for longer than an hour, and then he was off again, through the evening and into the night, then into the black hours before dawn. His horses stumbled and gasped for air. Dinadan knew that he should rest them, but he could not escape the thought that Iseult's assassins might at that very moment be nearing Brangienne. He pushed his horses on, trying to stay in the centre of the forest path, praying that his horses would make it.

They did not. In a black patch of shadow beneath huge old trees at the heart of the forest, Dinadan missed the path, and his mount tripped. Down they rolled, the pack horse tumbling over them both. The horses scrambled to their feet again, which meant that they were not seriously injured, but when Dinadan heard their hoarse gasps for air, he knew he could ride them no further that night. He walked over to them, singing to them a soothing song and patting their noses gently. Only when their breath started to grow more even did he reach up on the saddle to make sure his rebec had survived the tumble. To his relief, he found it whole, and then he had an idea.

Taking the rebec from his saddle, he tuned it swiftly, then began to play. He played as loudly and as sharply as he could, trying to capture in his music his own sense of urgency. The tune he played was an old ballad that he had learned first from Thomas the Rhymer, but even the venerable Thomas would have had trouble recognising the melody in the rapid, frantic rendition that Dinadan played. He played for about ten minutes, though it seemed longer as he listened eagerly to every forest sound, but at last his ears were rewarded with a faint whistle that grew stronger every moment, keeping time to Dinadan's dancing bow. A minute more, and the piping sound was just behind him, and Dinadan played a final flourish, then stopped.

"You called, Dinadan?" came a familiar voice.

"Yes, though I hardly dared hope that you would hear, Sylvanus," Dinadan replied.

"You are in need?"

Dinadan nodded. "I must get to the castle of King Isbaddadon. It means the life of a friend there."

"Tell me."

Dinadan took a breath. "Her name is Lady Brangienne. She alone knows a secret about Queen Iseult of Cornwall, and so she has been hiding from the queen these three years and more. But now Iseult knows where to find her, and I must warn Brangienne before any harm can come to her."

Sylvanus was silent for a moment, then said, "You may relax. Iseult has sent messengers, but they are at the moment very lost indeed. They cannot arrive at Isbaddadon's court before tomorrow night." Dinadan sighed with relief. Sylvanus spoke again, "How is it that Queen Iseult has only now discovered the Lady Brangienne's hiding place?"

Dinadan didn't hesitate. "It was my fault. I was inquiring after her health from one who had been at the court, but I was careless in speaking her name publicly. Please, Sylvanus, if Iseult's men are still a day away from the court, how close am I?"

"Not ten minutes, my friend," came the reply, and as the forest sprite finished speaking, the shadows around them seemed to begin moving. Dinadan stared until his eyes hurt, but all he could ever say afterwards was that it appeared that the world itself moved by him, and as he and his horses stood still, Isbaddadon's castle came to him. At any rate, in a very few minutes, he stood outside the familiar gates of Isbaddadon's castle, unsure how it had happened, but grateful nonetheless.

It actually took Dinadan longer to gain admittance through the gate than it had taken him to arrive there from the woods, but at last a guard appeared who remembered Dinadan from his earlier visits years before, and Dinadan was allowed to bring his horses in. Once inside, though, Dinadan was unsure what to do. He meant to take Lady Brangienne away, and it seemed to him that his best chance was to do it during the night and avoid any contact with either Isbaddadon or Olwen, but he did not know where Lady Brangienne's bedchamber might be. Leaving his horses in the courtyard, he went to the only place he could think to go – the kitchens.

They were empty. Suddenly aware of his hunger, Dinadan helped himself to a slab of beef as he tried to remember which corridor Brangienne had always taken to return to her rooms after they had met here before. He was just reaching for a second slice, when a voice behind him said calmly, "I thought we'd seen the last of you. Missed our pantry, did you?"

Dinadan smiled and relaxed. Without turning around, he said, "Odd how every time I come to these kitchens I find you here." He took a bite of beef, then turned. Brangienne looked older, and somehow more serious, but her eyes were still lively and intelligent. "Well, you look all right. The past few years haven't been too hard on you, I hope."

Brangienne's eyes clouded. "I couldn't even tell you. What are you doing here?"

"I came to find you," Dinadan replied.

"How flattering," she replied at once. "To be so concerned for me – after not seeing me for three years and four months." Her tone was deeply sarcastic. "Suppose you tell me why you're really here."

Dinadan felt his face grow red. "I guess it has been too long. To tell you the truth, I've thought of you often enough these past years, but I couldn't bring myself to get mixed up in Culloch's stupidity again. I guess that's not very complimentary to you, is it? That I thought of you but wouldn't inconvenience myself to see you."

Brangienne hesitated. "No, it isn't," she said at last. "But I'd feel the same way. He truly is an absolute ass, and Olwen's just as bad. So, what brought you back now?"

Dinadan blinked, recalled suddenly to his

purpose. "I've come to take you away. Iseult knows you're here, and you're in danger."

Brangienne was silent for a long moment. At last she said, "Am I? I've been wondering about that. Does she still want me dead after all this time?"

"She's sent some soldiers to find you."

"Are you sure?"

"I trust the one who told me. He says they'll be here soon. You need to leave at once."

Brangienne's face was still. "How did she find out?" she asked suddenly.

Dinadan swallowed. "My fault. I was with a friend and we ran into Culloch. I asked about you, not thinking about the company. Then a day or two later we met Iseult, and my friend, in all innocence, mentioned you."

"You asked about me?" Brangienne repeated slowly. Dinadan shrugged. "And so then you came straight here to warn me?"

"I had to get here before Iseult's messengers did," Dinadan explained. "Iseult wasted no time in sending them, if they're already only a day away, which is what I was told."

"Who told you?"

Dinadan licked his lips once. "It's a bit hard to explain. He's not... well, I know he's someone to be trusted, but I can't —"

"Was it a shadowy person with horns?" Brangienne asked abruptly.

Dinadan nodded, his eyes on Brangienne's face. "Do you know Sylvanus?"

"Is that his name? No. No, I don't. But the reason I'm here tonight was because someone like that woke me and sent me downstairs. It seems that I had better leave." Her voice was remarkably calm, Dinadan thought, as if she were planning to run a minor errand instead of leave the place where she had lived for more than three years. Her eyes met his. "But where?"

Dinadan replied. "I thought I'd take you to Arthur's court," he said.

"No." Her voice was still calm, almost matter-of-fact.

"No?"

"No," Brangienne replied decidedly. "You can't know what it's like, being a lady-in-waiting: your life devoted to helping foolish women do all the things that are most likely to keep them foolish. I want no more of courts."

"Then... then where? I don't know of any other place of safety."

"How about a convent?" Brangienne asked.

"A convent? You?"

Brangienne smiled. "Don't think I'm being

rash. I've been planning this for ages. I dream every night of leaving this place, but I will not leave just to go to another like it. I want to be with people of sense, which means I should be with women, but not with noblewomen. Do you know any convents we could get to in a day or two?"

Dinadan thought for a moment. "I know an abbey – St Anselm's – and one of the monks there is a friend. He might know of a convent. How long will it take you to pack?"

Brangienne almost laughed. "I've been packed for three years now. Are your horses in the courtyard? I'll meet you there."

And so it was that a week later, having followed Brother Eliot's directions to the Sisters of Joy Convent, Dinadan delivered Brangienne to a fierce-looking woman with heavy jowls and thick eyebrows under an imposing wimple. The nun took Brangienne in without a murmur, but glared at Dinadan as if he were a murderer. Dinadan blinked at the woman's glare and said mildly, "You're sure about this, Brangienne?"

Brangienne looked at Dinadan, and her face softened. "I'll be all right, Dinadan. Thank you." Then she went inside, her fine gown ridiculously out of place beside her escort's plain habit, and the gates closed behind her.

8

THE HORN OF IGRAINE

While Dinadan was not completely comfortable leaving Brangienne with that scowling nun, it seemed likely that she was safe for the time being. But if Iseult was going to keep looking for her, then that safety was only temporary. Dinadan had been considering the matter, and now he knew what he had to do. If Iseult wanted Brangienne dead in order to conceal the story of the magic potion, then he had to show her that killing her would make matters worse. Dinadan headed back toward Tintagel.

About noon on his fourth day of travelling, as he retraced his steps back to Cornwall, he heard a familiar sound, an odd, melodic strumming. Dinadan stopped abruptly. "Palomides?" he called. The music stopped, and a moment later

Palomides appeared from a camp in the trees.

"Is it you indeed, my friend? I am overjoyed," the Moor said.

"What are you doing here? Didn't you go to Camelot?" Dinadan asked, dismounting and embracing the Moor.

"No, my friend. Before I had gone a furlong I realised that I did not wish to continue without you." Dinadan blinked, then smiled. "So, my friend, I have been waiting for you," Palomides explained.

"But how did you know I'd be coming back this way?"

"I did not know, of course, but it was reasonable. Something that Queen Iseult said sent you away with an urgent message. I decided that something so urgent would probably bring you back to see her again." Dinadan was silent, and Palomides added, "I do not ask what it was."

Dinadan nodded. "Yes, and thank you for that, but I think I should trust you. You see, it wasn't something Iseult said that sent me away, but something *I* said, about Lady Brangienne. The reason that Iseult wants to find her is to keep her from telling a secret. Brangienne has been in hiding from Iseult for three years, but through my own carelessness, Iseult learned her whereabouts."

Palomides's jaw tightened. "But it was I who

told this to Queen Iseult. Did I indeed put a lady's life in danger?"

"You weren't to know," Dinadan said. "But it's all right now. Brangienne's safe in a different place."

Palomides's eyes were hot. "I do not like to give aid, even unwittingly, to the wicked," he said sternly. "You go to Queen Iseult now?"

Dinadan nodded. "I'm going to tell her that I know her secret, too, and that if anything happens to Brangienne, I'll tell everyone in England." They stood silent for a moment, then Dinadan shook off his solemnity. "But there's no need for you to go along. After all, you're looking for great knights, and all they've got at Tintagel is Tristram."

"Perhaps I may find another," Palomides replied calmly. "Allow me to saddle my horse."

And so they rode together toward Tintagel, taking turns playing and singing.

They were only an hour from Tintagel when they came upon a knight resting in a clearing beside the road. As was his practice with every knight they met, Palomides rode up to meet him, and so by the time Dinadan recognised Sir Lamorak it was too late to turn away. "Blast," Dinadan muttered.

Palomides glanced at Dinadan. "What is wrong, my friend?... Oh, I see."

"Hello, friend knights," Sir Lamorak said, striding forward and smiling pleasantly.

They stopped their horses. "Good day, Sir Lamorak," Dinadan said.

Sir Lamorak frowned. "Do I know you?" he asked with surprise.

"I couldn't say," Dinadan said. "My name is Dinadan, and this is Sir Palomides."

Sir Lamorak stared, as everyone did, at Palomides's dark skin. "But I have seen you before! I was engaged in mortal combat with Sir Tristram and a dark-skinned knight rode up and watched! Surely it was you, Sir Palomides."

"It was," Palomides replied evenly. "I am impressed that even in such a battle as that you were aware of our arrival."

"Are you friends of Sir Tristram's?" Sir Lamorak asked abruptly.

"No," Palomides and Dinadan replied together.

Sir Lamorak smiled again, at least with his lips, and said, "That's too bad. You see I am looking for friends of Tristram's who might deliver a message to him."

"Bad luck," Dinadan replied. "Keep looking, though. Tristram must have a friend somewhere."

Sir Lamorak ignored him. "But maybe you could help anyway," he continued. "You see, I've been feeling bad about always fighting with Sir Tristram over whose lady is fairest."

"You should," Palomides replied. "To squabble like a child over your lady's reputation only stains it."

Sir Lamorak's lips tightened, but then he smiled weakly. "As you say. So, because I feel so bad, I want to make amends. I have a gift for Queen Iseult. I don't suppose you're on your way to Tintagel, are you?"

"We are," said Palomides.

"What good luck! Do you think you could deliver this present for me? I'm not sure that I'd be allowed in, you see, what with Tristram being there and all. Here, let me show it to you." He reached into his pack and produced a silver horn that shone with faint, greenish light. "This is a magic horn, from the faery beauty whom I love. She says it was charmed by the great enchantress Igraine herself, and she sends it with her compliments. Its magic is such that any noble soul who drinks from it will double in beauty after one drink."

"What if your soul isn't noble?" Dinadan asked, sceptical. It didn't seem a very suitable gift for Iseult.

Sir Lamorak smiled again. "My lady sends this horn expressly for Queen Iseult, and she knows best what it will do. Please, would you deliver it for me?"

"We do not go to give gifts," Palomides said.

179

"But couldn't you take it along anyway?" Sir Lamorak pleaded. "I promised my lady that I would send it to her, and how shall I do so if you will not help me?"

Sir Lamorak's voice was plaintive, and Dinadan wrinkled his nose with distaste, but Palomides only sighed softly. "For the sake of your promise, I will," he said and took the horn.

It was evening when they arrived at Tintagel. Palomides stopped his horse before the great castle gates and demanded the right of a knight errant to gain entrance. The gates opened to them. They rode together into the castle, surrendered their horses to an elderly groom, and were informed that the king and queen were at dinner. The knights hesitated, but a steward assured them that King Mark had standing orders that wandering knights should be shown to him immediately upon their arrival.

"Very hospitable," Palomides said, but Dinadan was not so sure.

The steward took them to the banquet room, and Palomides and Dinadan stepped unannounced into the hall. Servants bustled about with trays of food, and a dozen or so knights and ladies sat at a long banquet table. At its head was a pale, thin man wearing a large and heavy-looking crown that came so far down his head that it covered his eyebrows and rested on his ears. King Mark, Dinadan decided. At the foot of the table sat Iseult, and beside her was Tristram.

"Why, hello!" Tristram exclaimed, standing and gazing at Palomides. He started forward, as if to welcome the travellers. "Fancy seeing you again. Sir Dinomides, isn't it?"

"I'll welcome my own guests, Tristram," King Mark said querulously. He sounded as thin and sickly as he looked. "Well? What do you want?" he demanded.

"Yes, that's a much better welcome," Dinadan murmured to himself. He bowed slightly and said in a louder voice, "Good evening, your highness. I am Sir Dinadan, of King Arthur's court, and this is my friend Sir Palomides."

"Friend, is he?" King Mark replied. "Looked like a deuced Moor, to me."

Palomides made no reply, and Dinadan said as gently as he could, "He *is* a Moor, which would account for his looking like one."

King Mark's eyes narrowed, but all he said was, "Well?"

"With your highness's permission, I have come with a private message for Queen Iseult. I am sorry that we have interrupted your dinner, though, and I would be happy to wait until you are done to give it."

"A private message?" King Mark asked. His eyes were tiny slits now.

"I do not permit it!" declared Tristram suddenly.

King Mark focused his suspicious eyes on Tristram now. "You do not permit it?" he repeated.

Tristram lifted his chin. "The queen and I have no secrets."

King Mark started to turn red, and Iseult said, "Be quiet, Sir Tristram."

"Have you not?" King Mark said, through clenched teeth. "And have the two of you no secrets from me?"

Iseult's eyes opened wide, and she assumed the childish voice that she had used on Palomides and Dinadan back on the trail. "But of courthe not, my lord. Why, whatever could you mean?"

For several seconds King Mark glared silently at Iseult and Tristram, while the rest of the lords and ladies of the court gazed at their plates without moving. Watching them, Dinadan concluded that they were used to such exchanges as these and had developed the ability to fade into the background and draw no attention to themselves. Very like hedgehogs, he thought.

Palomides spoke for the first time. "If it please your highness, we mean no disrespect to you or to the queen. We merely bear some news for her concerning her former maid, Lady Brangienne. It is of no interest to anyone but the queen, and if we may tell her, we shall leave at once and bother you no further."

At Brangienne's name Iseult glanced up eagerly. "Ith she dead?"

Dinadan felt a twinge of nausea, but he took a breath and said, "That's the matter I want to talk to you about."

Iseult started to stand, but King Mark interrupted. "No one speaks to my wife without my permission!"

Tristram raised one hand placatingly and said to the king, "Here's a solution that will make everyone happy. Why don't these knights give their message to me, and then I'll tell Iseult later, when we're alone."

"Ssh, Tristram!" Iseult hissed. King Mark looked at the queen and at Tristram, his face turning red and a vein bulging in his neck.

"You have no reason to be alone with my wife! And as for you two," the king roared at Palomides and Dinadan, "get out!"

Iseult caught Dinadan's eye and favored him with a series of winks and nods and odd grimaces. She looked as if she were having a mild fit, but Dinadan guessed she was trying to convey a message, probably to wait for her outside. Dinadan glanced at Palomides. "Come on. Let's go."

"No," he said. "We must speak to Queen Iseult. And besides, we have that gift to give her."

Iseult smiled brightly. "A gift? You brought a gift for me?"

"I forbid you to give my wife a gift!" King Mark shouted.

"It is not from us," Palomides said calmly. He produced the magic horn. "This is a gift from Sir Lamorak and from his lady. Sir Lamorak begs pardon from the queen for having slighted her beauty and offers her the Horn of Igraine. The horn is said to be magical and to double the beauty of all who drink of it, provided their hearts are noble." Iseult squeaked excitedly, but Palomides ignored her. He set the horn on the table beside her, then looked up at King Mark. "I shall leave you to your dinner, but we will speak to your lady before we leave Tintagel."

The king did not respond. He was watching Iseult, who had eagerly snatched up the horn and filled it with wine from her own cup. "Double beauty!" she said breathlessly, raising the cup to her lips.

Wine splattered everywhere, splashing Iseult's face and dribbling in a stream over the front of her gown. Iseult screamed with annoyance and anger. "Who jostled me?" she demanded. A drop of wine

184

trembled at the end of her nose, then fell. "I'll have your head for this, whoever it was. Who did it?"

"No one touched you," Palomides said calmly, but Iseult didn't hear.

"Look at my dress! Ruined! The whole cup of wine spilled. I didn't even get a taste!"

"Waste of good wine," Dinadan murmured.

Several ladies had rushed to the queen's assistance and were ineffectually dabbing at her stained gown with their handkerchiefs. Iseult continued scolding, and Dinadan watched the scene with interest. While Iseult was preoccupied, one of the ladies gently took the horn from Iseult's hand and surreptitiously filled it from a flagon of wine. Evidently, she thought to double her own beauty while she had the chance. She lifted the horn to her lips, and the wine poured itself down her chin and breast. She shrieked with dismay, attracting Iseult's attention. Iseult screamed even louder. "That's mine! Give it back!"

With one hand, Iseult snatched the horn away from the lady, and with the other she grabbed the lady's hair and began to pull it vigorously.

Palomides turned away, disgusted, but Dinadan watched the melée with growing appreciation. Iseult appeared frail and ethereal but was evidently stronger than she looked. No one could break her grip either on her lady's hair or on the faery horn.

"It's mine, it's mine, it's mine!" she rapped out. In the middle of the knot of tugging women was Tristram, himself liberally spattered with wine, trying helplessly to disentangle himself.

A low laugh came from the great doors behind King Mark's seat, and all the company turned to see a beautiful woman, splendidly clad in a gown that glowed with an eerie light, standing just inside the hall. The ladies, occupied with each other's hair and eyes, were the last to notice the visitor, but once they saw her, even they grew still. Iseult stopped screaming and pulling, though her hand remained twined in her lady's hair. "I see you've received my gift," the woman said with an evil smile. No one spoke, and after a moment, the woman said, "But perhaps my young lover did not completely explain its magic, for I see no reason to fight over it. Indeed, I hope that all this court might drink of it."

The woman paced majestically forward until she was beside King Mark. "Know this, O king. That horn is a test. Only the one who is faithful in love may drink from it. If anyone who is unfaithful tries to drink, the wine will spill out and stain the drinker."

"What?" King Mark roared. His vein was bulging again.

Iseult's eyes widened as she looked at King Mark. "You... you don't bewieve thith woman, do you, my wuv?"

"I knew it!" King Mark shouted. "It's that Tristram, isn't it? You think you were clever, but I'm no fool!"

"No, no!" Iseult said earnestly. "You mutht be imagining things!"

The lady whose hair Iseult still held said sharply, "Well, if he is, then so is everyone else. For heaven's sake, everyone knows about your affair with Tristram!"

King Mark turned purple and Tristram pushed himself forward. "That's impossible!" he declared. "I haven't told a soul!"

Iseult shrieked, "You idiot!" and King Mark began to rave incoherently, hopping up and down. He was joined in his fury by one of the knights sitting beside him, apparently the husband of the second stained lady. He had evidently just grasped the implications of the horn's magic for himself, and was no better pleased than the king. Dinadan looked at Tristram and shook his head, wondering how he could possibly be related to this clodpole.

"You trollop!" the knight beside King Mark shouted. "Who is it? Who have you been dallying with? Mother told me you were no good!"

"They're *all* trollops!" King Mark shrieked, beside himself. "All women are false! They shall all drink from the horn! Every one! Who shall be first?"

There was a general cry of dismay from the ladies and from some of the men, who begged the king to make no rash decisions. Several ladies began edging toward the door, and one fainted, or pretended to. King Mark and the other husband continued to rant, Iseult and her spattered lady to plead, and Tristram to look confused for several minutes, and in the hubbub Dinadan noticed that the faery beauty had disappeared.

King Mark appeared to be set on taking his revenge on the whole company by forcing every lady in the room to drink from the horn, and was even starting to line them up, when Palomides, his face in grim disgust, stepped forward and took the horn from the table. "Stop this foolishness," he said evenly.

The vein in King Mark's throat bulged again, larger than ever. Dinadan watched its pounding with interest, then said, "I believe you're about to go off in an apoplexy, your highness. Not that I'm opposed to it, mind, but I thought you'd want to know."

King Mark ignored him. "Do you dare oppose my will?" he demanded of Palomides.

Palomides met the king's eyes, and the king's gaze dropped at once. "I dare," Palomides replied. "If you are set on forcing the ladies to drink from this horn, then it is fitting that the men should drink as well.

And as king, it would be your place to drink first."

The hall grew still, and for the first time in a quarter of an hour, the king ceased gobbling in rage. His eyes grew wide.

Palomides waited until there was no sound at all, then he dropped the horn on the stone floor and stepped on it. It crushed under his heel, and he ground it to dust, then turned and strode out of the hall.

Dinadan stepped close to Iseult, smiled pleasantly, and said, "Always getting yourself in trouble by drinking the wrong thing, aren't you?"

It took Iseult a moment, but then she understood, and she turned horrified eyes toward Dinadan.

"That's right," Dinadan said softly. "I know all about that potion on the ship. And, if anything happens to Lady Brangienne, I shall tell the tale to everyone in England. Do you understand me?" Iseult did not move, and Dinadan stopped smiling. Leaning forward until he was inches from Iseult's face, he repeated, "Do you understand me?"

Iseult nodded.

"That's the dandy," Dinadan said, smiling again. He turned his attention again to King Mark, whose face was still purple and who seemed to be having trouble breathing. "Thank you for a very pleasant evening, your highness. I had a lovely time." Then he left, closing the door gently behind him.

9

THE BALLAD OF

SIR PALOMIDES

Dinadan caught up with Palomides in the courtyard, and they rode out of Tintagel together. The Moor seemed preoccupied, so Dinadan respected his mood and did not speak for several miles. At last, the summer sun being about to set, Dinadan asked mildly, "Are we going to stop for the night?"

"If you wish, my friend," Palomides replied.

Dinadan nodded. "I usually do," he said.

They made camp in a wide, treeless meadow. They had travelled together enough that they had a routine and were able to care for their horses and make a light supper without talking, but when they had eaten, Palomides leaned back against his saddle and spoke. "Are Sir Tristram and Sir Lamorak truly considered great knights?"

"By some."

"But they are fools and villains."

"Well, yes, if you want to quibble," Dinadan said.

"I thought I knew what a knight was when I came here, but now I do not. I see such different examples before me. Please, my friend, can you tell me what makes a man a knight?"

Dinadan hesitated, remembering with shame how he had been knighted at his father's drunken hands. "I don't think I can," he said at last. He let his breath out slowly. "There was some Greek who said that everything on earth is just a reflection of the perfect, ideal form of that thing. I forget the fellow's name."

"Plato," Palomides said. "I'm surprised that the English have heard of him."

Dinadan grinned. "King Arthur reads a lot, and he mentioned him one time. Anyway, I think about this notion of ideals sometimes. Is there an ideal figure of a knight? The eternal knight that every earthly knight is supposed to reflect?"

"Yes!" Palomides said. "That's just what I want to know."

"I don't think there is," Dinadan said bluntly. "Everyone has a different notion of what a knight is, and so everyone is imitating a different imagined ideal. Tristram and Lamorak think the perfect knight is a great fighter who fetches sticks for his lady love. Others think the true knight's the one who wins the most tournaments, or who wears the dandiest clothes. And heaven only knows what Culloch would think a knight is, if Culloch had a brain to think with."

Palomides frowned. "But if every knight makes up his own idea of what a knight is, how does one judge? How can I know what a great knight is like?"

"You should meet Arthur and Gawain and Bedivere," Dinadan said. "Then you would see what knights should be. So, since we've done spreading cheer at Tintagel, shall we go to Camelot?"

The Moor looked at Dinadan for a long, silent minute, his eyes intense in the firelight and shaded with thought. Then Palomides said, "Very well. But not at once. I think, my lord Dinadan, that I should like to see more of Britain – if you would accompany me."

Dinadan was puzzled by, but not averse to, the suggestion. He meant to ride back to the convent and check on Brangienne in a few months, after she'd had some time to settle in, but he had no plans in the meantime. "Ever see Scotland?" he asked.

The two knights rode together for two months, to

Scotland and Orkney and then south again. Occasionally they met other knights and often encountered minstrels. It was from the minstrels that Dinadan heard the results of his and Palomides's visit to Tintagel. King Mark, mad with jealous rage, had confined Iseult to the castle, and she was locked in a tower bedroom after dark. All passing knights were turned away at the gates. As for Tristram, it was reported that he was wandering about England, unwashed and unkempt, eating roots and challenging everyone he met to battle. Everyone said he'd been driven mad by love, like someone in a bad story. Dinadan had never believed such tales, but if anyone's mind was weak enough to be overset by such a thing as love, it would be Tristram's.

One crisp autumn day, the two knights came upon the sort of mysterious encounter that always seemed to lead to adventure in knightly tales. Topping a hill, they saw a black barge, tied at the edge of a wide river, and beside the barge, an armoured knight with a grey beard kneeling before a rough wooden cross.

As the two knights approached, the knight looked up, and his eyes were weary with grief. He did not speak, but he rose to his feet, drew his sword, and laid it on the ground. "At last," the man said. "I am ready."

Dinadan and Palomides glanced at each other. Dinadan shrugged and said, "Ready for what?"

"I will not resist you," the man said. "I have been apart from my brother for too long, and I am ready to rejoin him."

Dinadan scratched his chin and looked again at Palomides. The Moor didn't speak, but only frowned and looked past the man, at the barge. At last, feeling he ought to say something, Dinadan said, "Right, then. Go see your brother. We wouldn't dream of stopping you."

The old man looked at Dinadan, and said in an anguished voice, "Must you sport with me, too? Did your masters Helius and Helake bid you mock me first?"

Dinadan blinked and started to protest, but Palomides spoke. "Is that your brother in the boat, my lord?" he asked. Dinadan looked again and realized that the boat was a funeral barge. As a breeze shook the drapes, he glimpsed inside the body of a white-haired man.

"Yes," the old man said. "That is King Hermance. I beg you to delay no more, but do what you were sent to do." With that, the old man bowed his head and bared his neck.

"He expects us to kill him," Palomides said to Dinadan.

"Some people are so demanding," Dinadan replied. "Considering we've only just met, I mean."

The old man looked up, puzzlement in his face. "Do you mean you aren't from Helius and Helake either?"

"No," Dinadan said. "Who are they?"

The man sighed and shook his head sadly. "I must say, it's the outside of enough. I get myself all ready, and then nothing comes of it after all, and I have to start again."

Palomides dismounted. "But forgive me, my lord, why do you wish to die?"

"Oh, it's not that I wish it. It's just that I won't leave my brother again, and so my death is inevitable. Helius and Helake can't leave me alive, or their throne would be unsafe."

Dinadan dismounted beside Palomides. "It sounds like a story. We've nothing very pressing just now. Why don't you tell us what this is about? Who are Helius and Helake?"

The lines on the man's face eased, and he nodded. "My nephews," he said. "Or step-nephews, rather. Twin boys that my brother, the King of Withernsea, took in as his own after their parents were drowned in a flood."

"That was decent of him," Dinadan commented.

"There was no man more kind and good than

195

Hermance," the man said. "It was what made him so fit to be king, and what made me so unfit to take his place. I never had his patience or goodness."

"But why should you have taken his place anyway?" Palomides asked.

"Hermance never had children, you see. And then, when his wife died and he swore that he'd never marry again, it didn't take a wizard to see who was up next. Hermance began to groom me for the throne, and I wanted none of it. I wanted adventure. So I left. That was more than twenty years ago."

"Did you find adventure?" Dinadan asked.

"No," the man said grimly. "Nor does anyone else. Adventure is something that happens to someone else. When it's happening to you, it's only trouble."

"You found something better than adventure," Palomides said gravely. "You found wisdom. Perhaps you would not be such a bad king after all."

The man shook his head briskly, as if driving away a fly, and said, "It hardly mattered, though. Shortly after I left, Hermance took in these two peasant boys, who had been found by a boatman, and raised them up to be his heirs." The man shook his head slowly. "He seems to have made a wretched business of it, too. I can see what happened, of course. Hermance was always quick to sympathise

196

with the unfortunate, and he must have given the orphan boys everything they wanted and more."

Dinadan nodded with understanding. "Probably not the best way to groom wise and generous kings, you mean?"

"They became evil, grasping men, taking what they wanted from the land and the people, abusing every right and privilege they had been given. They became so brazen that word of their deeds spread beyond Withernsea, and I heard of them. I came home. But too late." He looked back over his shoulder at the funeral barge.

"What happened?" Palomides asked.

"I don't know. Perhaps Hermance confronted his adopted sons. Perhaps they were just tired of him. But they killed him and threw the body in the Humber River." He looked up, frowning with pain. "Why the river? Why would they do that?"

"Is this the same river in which their true parents drowned?" Palomides asked.

"Yes," the old man said. "The same river that they should have drowned in themselves!"

"How did King Hermance end up on the boat?" Dinadan asked gently.

"There is a boatman who lives near the castle, a good man. It was he who found Helius and Helake and brought them to my brother. It was also he who, twenty years later, found my brother's body. Then the boatman did a brave thing: he decided the people of Withernsea should know what had happened. He turned his own boat into this sad funeral barge and poled it up river, crying out for all to come and see their murdered king."

"I should like to meet this boatman," Palomides said.

The old man gestured to the rough cross where he knelt. "This is his grave. He got this far up the river before the brothers' soldiers caught up with him. They shot him with arrows and were about to hang him, still alive, when I arrived here. I stopped the hanging, and drove the men away. The good boatman lived long enough to tell me his story. I have stayed here since then, waiting."

Dinadan frowned. "Waiting for what? Oh... I see. You told the men who were killing the boatman who you were, didn't you?"

The old man nodded. "Yes. I told them to leave in the name of Hermind, Prince of Withernsea – that's my name. It wasn't the cleverest thing I could have done, I've realised. That was the day before yesterday. Helius and Helake will be sending someone soon, I should think."

Dinadan and Palomides looked at each other in silence for a moment, then Dinadan sighed. "I suppose I ought to put on my blasted armour. Hope it still fits."

The assassins came later that day, seven mounted knights. Dinadan watched them approach, and though his heart was pounding with nervousness, he spoke casually, "You must have a fierce reputation, Hermind, for the brothers to send such a crowd."

"No," Palomides said. "It is a sign of their fear. Only cowards would send seven against one. Come, friends." He mounted his horse. Dinadan supposed Palomides would consider him a coward, too, if the Moor knew how little he wanted to fight, but he followed Palomides's example.

The seven knights rode down the hill to the river, then stopped. One said, "Which of you is Hermind the Usurper?"

Sir Hermind drew his sword. "I am Sir Hermind, brother of the good king Hermance, who lies dead here, murdered by those he loved, but I am no usurper."

"Who are these others?" the knight demanded. His voice cracked slightly.

Palomides answered. "Today, we are all Hermind. To kill him, you must kill us all."

The knight hesitated. "We... we only

intended… no one said there were three of you!"

Palomides charged, and the other two followed. Dinadan managed to draw his sword without cutting off his horse's ears, and even landed one glancing blow on a knight's hand, making that knight drop his sword and jerk backwards, so sharply that he fell from his horse, but beyond that he contributed little to the ensuing fray. He didn't need to do more, though. Sir Hermind unseated two of the attacking knights, and Palomides appeared to be quite competent to take on the remaining four himself. Dinadan had never seen Palomides fight, but the Moor was a warrior of great skill. In no time at all, only one of the original seven was still mounted and that was only because he was galloping away with all the speed his horse could muster.

Palomides dismounted and stood amid the six fallen knights. Three were obviously dead, but the others were stirring. Palomides selected the one who seemed least injured – the one Dinadan had bashed on the knuckles – and jerked him to his feet. "Where are your masters?" the Moor asked sternly.

"My… my masters?"

Palomides gave the knight a casual cuff in the helm with the back of his gauntlet, and the knight staggered backwards and dropped to one knee. "Your masters, Helius and Helake," Palomides said.

"I don't know what —" Palomides stepped forward and raised his gauntlet again. "They're at Withernsea Castle, your honour, waiting for us," the knight said hurriedly.

"Take us to them," Palomides said.

The knight dropped to his other knee. "I can't!" he said plaintively. "They'll kill me!"

"Very well," Palomides said. He turned to Dinadan and Sir Hermind. "Friends, this man came to commit murder. What is your judgment?"

"Death," Sir Hermind said grimly.

"Seems fair enough," agreed Dinadan.

Palomides lifted his sword, and the knight said, "I'll take you to them, if you like."

They rode toward Withernsea Castle two by two, with Palomides and their captive in the lead. Sir Hermind, who seemed much younger than he had before the battle, lifted his chin and said to Dinadan, "I don't know what I would have done had you and your friend not come along when you did."

"I'm glad we did," Dinadan murmured politely. "Lucky thing, too. What were the chances of two knights arriving just when you needed some help?"

"That is indeed amazing, for in truth you were not even the first knights to come to me as I waited for death."

Dinadan raised one eyebrow. "You mean someone else came along before we did?" Sir Hermind nodded, and Dinadan frowned. "Well, what happened to him?"

"He went away again."

"Didn't you tell him your story?" Dinadan asked.

"Most of it," Sir Hermind replied, "but when I told him how Helius and Helake had usurped the throne, this knight said he wouldn't help. He said it was not fitting for a true knight to fight against the peasant-born."

"Silly ass," Dinadan commented. "It's true that Arthur tells his knights not to raise arms against peasants, but to leave you to die for such a scruple... What an idiot that knight must be. You didn't catch his name, did you?"

Sir Hermind shook his head. "No, but he was very strange. His eyes were never still, and even as we talked he muttered to himself and twice pulled his sword to defend himself against enemies that he alone could see. And though he talked much, he said that he could not speak."

Dinadan closed his eyes. "Because he'd taken a vow of silence?"

"Why, yes. Do you know this knight?"

"It doesn't matter," Dinadan replied. "Tell me, Sir Hermind, have you thought about what we'll do once we get to the castle? I mean, what'll you do with the brothers?"

Sir Hermind's brow contracted. At length he said, "When I first came back, it was with the idea that I might somehow convince Helius and Helake that their tyranny had to stop, but that's no good anymore, is it? I mean, after they killed Hermance, they couldn't remain on the throne at all, could they?" Dinadan shook his head. Sir Hermind frowned more deeply. "I don't know."

"Worth thinking about," Dinadan said, adding cheerfully, "Of course, it may not matter; they may kill us."

Withernsea Castle was a towering fortress, with high ramparts that seemed to rise right out of the Humber River itself. It was built into a bend in the river, so that the river bounded the castle on two sides, and a wide canal had been dug around the other two sides, leaving the castle on an island. It would be nearly impossible to force an entrance, but oddly enough the drawbridge over the canal was down, and the gate open.

"There it is, your honour," Palomides's captive said. "Please don't make me go any further. The brothers have their throne room in that corner tower there, where they can see almost the whole kingdom. You'll find them soon enough without me."

Palomides nodded in dismissal, and the captive knight wheeled his horse and rode away as fast as he could. Palomides looked at the others. "It is strange that the gates are open. Is it a trap?"

"Probably," Dinadan said. "Does it make any difference?"

Palomides shook his head. "No. Whether a trap or no, we should never get into the castle otherwise. I say we cross now and take the adventure that befalls us."

"Off we go, then," Dinadan said, assuming a cheerfulness he didn't feel. They rode into the castle.

It was nearly deserted. The three dismounted and, drawing their swords, began looking around. A few servants passed them, but these showed no surprise at three armed knights roaming the castle halls and courts. Eventually they found the long, winding stair that led to the throne room, and they climbed the tower.

The throne room was nearly bare. In it was only a single wooden throne, with its high back to the door, facing a large window. The three stood at the door for a moment, wondering where to look next, when a voice came from the other side of the throne. "Come in, come in."

"Are you Helius and Helake?" Sir Hermind asked.

"I'm one of them," the voice replied. "Come

around here where I can see you."

Sir Hermind and Palomides walked around the throne and turned to face the one seated on it. Dinadan, though, did not move. "Where is your brother?" Palomides asked.

The voice from the throne said, "Now how should I know that? Am I my brother's keeper?" Keeping his feet in position, so as not to make any noise on the stone floor, Dinadan looked carefully around the throne room. It seemed odd to find only one of the brothers here; everyone who had mentioned them had always spoken of them together.

"Perhaps you do not care for your brother," Sir Hermind said. "But I care for mine. I am Hermind, brother of the good king Hermance, whom you killed."

The voice replied with a mocking tone. "Come for the funeral, did you?"

"You gave him no funeral."

"Not his funeral," the voice replied. "Yours."

There was a movement at the window that the throne faced, behind Palomides's and Sir Hermind's backs. Dinadan looked up to see a burly young man step around from the parapet to the window and draw back a wicked-looking boar spear, ready to impale Palomides from behind. Dinadan didn't stop to think. Dropping his sword, he lunged forward, roughly shouldering Sir Hermind into Palomides as he ran. Lowering his head, he threw himself forward into the man with the spear, and then they were both falling from the tower toward the river.

It was a long fall, quite long enough for Dinadan, unnaturally calm, to have several thoughts on the way. He hoped that the river was deep enough that they wouldn't just flatten themselves on the bottom, and then reflected that actually deep water wasn't much better, since he was in full armour and would sink like a rock. He wished with slight irritation that his companion on the fall would stop screaming so shrilly, and finally, just before hitting the water, he hoped that Brangienne was happy at the convent.

Dinadan's impact on the water was colossal. He would reflect later that in all likelihood he only survived the blow because of his armour, but it also knocked him completely unconscious. He had no memory from the moment of his hitting the water until he awoke some hours later on the bank of the river. It was dark, but the sky was clear and bright with stars, and against the sky Dinadan saw the dark outline of a slender, horned figure.

"Sylvanus?" he asked.

"It is good to see you again, my friend," the figure replied.

"Am I alive?"

"But of course. Else you would not be so sore."

Sylvanus was right. Every muscle ached fiercely. "But how? How did I survive the fall and the river?"

The outline of Sylvanus's cheek lifted slightly, and Dinadan knew the spirit was smiling. "The river didn't want you, my friend, but the one you brought with you. That one belonged to the river, and though it had been cheated of him once, many years ago, the river is patient. Perhaps it was grateful to you, and so it returned you to the air."

"Then I suppose I'm grateful, too. How is it that you're here? Just passing by?"

Sylvanus laughed, and his chuckle was music. "Hardly. I've been leading your friends' horses to you. They searched for you all afternoon, but were about to give up, so I had to help. Here they are now."

Sylvanus disappeared, and a minute later Dinadan heard riders approaching, speaking to each other in sombre tones. Recognising the voices of Palomides and Hermind, Dinadan struggled up onto one elbow. "I hope you brought my horses, too," he called out, "because I sure don't feel like walking."

Dinadan and Palomides stayed at Withernsea Castle for two weeks, long after Dinadan felt well enough to ride. He didn't even have any broken bones, but from the fuss that Sir Hermind and the castle servants made over him, you'd have thought he was at death's door. At last he convinced everyone that he was well enough to ride, and he and Palomides took their leave. Sir Hermind – or rather, King Hermind, now – tried once again to convince them to stay, and said for the thousandth time that he didn't deserve the kingship. After all, Dinadan had killed one brother, and Palomides the second – by grasping him in a rage and throwing him through the throne-room window after Dinadan and the first brother had gone over. (Dinadan never did learn whether it was Helius or Helake whom he had taken into the river, but it didn't seem to matter greatly.)

"But I tell you, you two were the ones who defeated the usurpers, so by rights you two should be kings instead of me."

"No true king is king by conquest," Palomides said. "You are king by right."

"But I never wanted to be king," Sir Hermind said.

"So much the better," replied Dinadan with a laugh. "After all, the brothers did want to be king and see what they were like? No, this is your home, not ours. Your place is at home." With that, the two friends mounted and rode away.

"So, where to?" Dinadan asked at last.

"As you said to Hermind," Palomides replied,

"home. It is time for me to return to Araby."

Startled, Dinadan looked at the Moor. "But what about Camelot? Weren't you going to go there to see the greatest knights in the land?"

Palomides reined in his horse and looked fondly at Dinadan. "I need not go to Camelot for that, my lord Dinadan. I have found what I came for, and now I may return. Will you ride with me to the coast?"

Stunned, Dinadan could only nod, and they turned south toward Dover.

They did not get very far together, though. Just a few hours later, they were accosted by a knight – a wild, unkempt knight in stained golden armour. Dinadan groaned softly. "Halt and fight, foul recreants!" Tristram shouted shrilly.

"No," Palomides replied disdainfully. He started to ride on.

"Then I shall slay you like dogs," Tristram screamed. He drew his sword and began to swing it wildly about his head.

"Put that down right now, Tristram," Dinadan said sternly. "For the sake of your mother, Lady Giselle of the Fens, put that sword away."

Tristram froze. "Mother?" He turned unblinking eyes toward Dinadan, then began to cry. "But I love her, Mother. And King Mark took her away, and now I have nothing." He lowered his sword.

Palomides looked curiously at Dinadan. "He is your brother," he said. It was not a question.

"Yes. A traitor and an ass and now a madman, but he's also my brother." Dinadan swallowed. "I'd better take him home."

"Then we will part now," Palomides said. He laid a hand on Dinadan's shoulder. "I will sing your songs in Araby."

Dinadan grinned. "And England will hear the Ballad of Sir Palomides."

10

THE LYRE

When Dinadan was a child, he had sometimes dreamed of a day when he would return to his home, side by side with his glorious older brother. By then, of course, they would both be celebrated knights, and their return would prompt cheers and adoration from all. He hadn't thought of that dream in years, not since his profane knighting at his father's hand and his subsequent oath never to return. It only went to show, he thought, how far one's dreams and intentions are from what one ends up doing. Here he was, returning home against his oath, but the return could hardly have been more different from his childhood dream. Dinadan returned as an attendant to a lunatic.

Tristram was obviously different, too. Except

that he still mumbled occasionally about a vow of silence, Dinadan would hardly have recognised his brother now. He was bearded, his hair long and unkempt, and his body pungently unwashed. He no longer moved with the grace of a natural athlete, but rather in short, jerky movements. His hands plucked with agitation at his armour, his saddle, his horse's mane, and at the hilt of his sword, which he unsheathed every two or three minutes. His eyes were either wide and empty, staring vacantly at the world around him, or else filled with tears or flitting nervously from side to side, as if every tree they passed were a hidden enemy.

Dinadan might never have been able to lead his nervous brother at all, had he not made the discovery that music soothed Tristram's distraction. And so, for mile after mile, Dinadan sat sideways in his saddle, improvising soothing melodies on his rebec. This treatment not only calmed Tristram for the moment, but it appeared to have a more permanent healing effect. After two days of travel, Tristram's movements were less restless and his eyes less vacant. As they sat around their fire on the third night, Tristram began to speak, and he sounded almost sane.

"Who are you, sir?" he asked suddenly.

Sane, but not necessarily smart. "My name

is Dinadan."

"I've heard that name before, I think."

"We've met several times, Sir Tristram, on different journeys."

"No, I mean a long time ago. Yes… that was my brother's name." Dinadan waited silently, not sure if he wanted to be recognised, but Tristram didn't make the connection. "I never really knew my brother," Tristram said slowly. "He was much younger, and all I could think of was knighthood and glory." Dinadan sighed. "I was going to be the greatest knight of all," Tristram continued. "But that was before Iseult." Tristram shook his head slowly. "I forgot all about honour and glory after that."

"Was she worth it?" Dinadan asked.

But the moment of lucidity had passed. An owl's hoot from the forest behind them made Tristram leap to his feet, sword in hand, and glare menacingly at the nothing that threatened. After a moment, Dinadan rolled up in his blankets and went to sleep.

Just before nightfall on the fourth day, they came to Fenton Village, not half an hour from Sir Meliodas's castle. They were almost home, but Dinadan would not pass through the village without stopping to call on his old friend and mentor, Thomas the Rhymer. Thomas lived with his son, a cooper, and though Dinadan had never been to Thomas's home, he had no trouble finding the cooper's shop, where a burly, middle-aged man was shaping laths for a barrel. "Good day, friend cooper," Dinadan said pleasantly. "Is this the home of Thomas the Rhymer?"

The cooper stood slowly and looked at Dinadan, then at Tristram, then at Dinadan again. "Ay, it used to be," he said. Dinadan looked a question, and the man said, "Are ye friends of my father's?"

"I am," Dinadan said. "Where is he? He's all right, I hope."

The cooper hesitated, then said, "Come inside, your worship. Have a quaff of ale with me, if you will."

"Gladly, friend," Dinadan said, dismounting. A slow certainty of grief began to grow within him. He followed the cooper into the rooms behind his shop, leaving Tristram outside with the horses. The cooper unstoppered a jug and poured two mugs of frothy brown ale, then raised his in an awkward toast. "He was a good man, was he not?"

Dinadan closed his eyes. "He's dead then?"

"Just over a year ago now."

Dinadan lifted his mug to the cooper's, and together they drank to the memory of one they both had loved. "I'm sorry," Dinadan said.

The cooper smiled. "Nay, it's not so bad as that. We've all to die, and Father died as he would have wanted, as if he'd writ the story of his own death."

"How did he die?"

"He was at the alehouse, singing a tale, and he just stopped once, asked a drink, then lay down at the table, and he was gone. His hands never let go his rebec, so we buried it with him."

Dinadan smiled. The cooper was right. It was a good way for Thomas to die. "What tale was he singing?" Dinadan asked.

The cooper smiled again. "His favourite one, in late years. The Noble Tale of Sir Dinadan."

Tears welled up in Dinadan's eyes, but his lips curved with delight. He put the cup down on the cooper's table. "I thank you for the drink, friend. Your father was the closest I had to a father, too. I am Sir Dinadan."

"I thought so. I saw the rebec on your saddle, and Father always said you were the best with an instrument he'd ever seen. It's why I asked you in. I've summat to give you." The cooper opened a cabinet, took out Thomas's old lyre, and gave it to Dinadan. "He said once he wished he'd given it to you before you left. I'd like you to take it."

The two sons of Thomas grinned at each other for a moment, but then the moment was spoiled.

Tristram poked his head into the room, then gasped. "A lyre!"

Annoyed, Dinadan glanced once at his brother. "That's right," he said abruptly.

"I used to play the lyre! Where did you get that?"

"It was a gift from this good man," Dinadan said.

Tristram stared at the cooper. "But you're a peasant! Why should a peasant have such a thing?"

Dinadan scowled, glanced apologetically at Thomas's son, then gently pushed Tristram back toward the horses. "It doesn't matter. Thank you for everything, my brother, but we have to be going if we're to make it to the castle before they close up. Sir Meliodas is still alive, I suppose?"

"Ay, last I heard." The cooper raised his hand in farewell, and Dinadan and Tristram rode away.

When they arrived, though, the castle was closed. They shouted and banged on the gates but could rouse no guards or servants. Near the top of the central keep, Dinadan saw a dimly lighted window, and once he heard the unmistakable sound of broken glass from the courtyard, as if someone had thrown a bottle from the upper window, but no one heard their calls, and at last Dinadan made camp outside the gates. He went to sleep dreading the prospect of the next morning's reunion with his father.

The reunion never happened. When Dinadan

awoke the next day, shortly before dawn, he realised that Tristram was gone. Somehow he had managed to get away with his horse and armour without waking Dinadan. He had taken something else, too: Thomas the Rhymer's lyre.

Dinadan arrived at Tintagel Castle several days later. Along the way, stopping at taverns and talking to people he met, he had heard reports of a bearded minstrel named Tramtris who played wearisome love songs on a lyre, but Dinadan hadn't needed those reports to know which direction Tristram had gone. As soon as he had noticed the missing lyre, he had known that Tristram was off to Iseult again.

Arriving at the gates and remembering that King Mark no longer admitted knights into the castle, Dinadan introduced himself as a minstrel. The guard snorted with disgust and said, "Go on with ye. We've already got an uncommon lot of minstrels here."

"I didn't know you could have too many minstrels," Dinadan ventured.

"Shows what you know," the guard replied. "We've only got one, and he's too much by half. All day long plucking at a harp and mooning around, with not a merry song to his name."

"What, you mean nothing like this?" Dinadan demanded, producing his rebec from its sling behind his saddle. He tuned it quickly, then sang for them his little song about ladies, and as he finished – "Which one is better to discard? The dragon or the damsel?" – the guard was guffawing loudly and opening the gate.

"Ay, you can come in. Now if that other blighter would leave, we'd be all right."

The "other blighter" was not hard to find. King Mark and Queen Iseult were in their throne room, and Tristram sat at their feet, plucking at the lyre and crooning a repetitive lyric in which "June" and "moon" figured prominently, alongside "love" and "dove" and "above". Dinadan was able to slip into the room unnoticed behind a small group of courtiers and to examine the scene carefully. It seemed that Tristram's beard and dishevelled appearance had been enough to disguise his identity from King Mark, but the glow in Iseult's eyes as she gazed at the minstrel "Tramtris" showed clearly that she knew him.

Dinadan had no desire to expose his brother, but neither did he intend to leave without recovering Thomas's lyre. He pushed his way through the collected courtiers and waited until Tristram finished his song. It lasted for several more stanzas, in which "tears" joined with "fears" and "heart" with "never apart". At last the song ended, and a sigh of relief filled the room. Dinadan stepped forward and cleared his throat. "Excuse me, your highness."

Mark looked up. "You! You're one of those who brought that blasted horn to my court!"

Dinadan nodded. "Well, yes. I did. But I didn't know what it was, remember."

"How dare you come back here!"

"I won't stay long, your highness I promise," Dinadan replied soothingly. "I've just come to get that lyre from the minstrel Tramtris."

A man's voice from the back of the room said distinctly, "Hear, hear!"

"No!" Tristram said.

"Yes," Dinadan said firmly. "It's mine, a gift from an old friend. You stole it from my things. Now give it to me, please."

"Hear, hear!" came the voice again. There was a murmur of approval from the court.

"You say that this minstrel stole this instrument from you?" King Mark asked. Dinadan nodded, and the king continued, "Then he must be punished."

"Hear, hear!"

"Off with his head," came a new voice.

Iseult frowned and said quickly, "You don't

execute someone for stealing a lyre!"

"How about for something else, then?"

"Anything!"

"Hear, hear!"

"Besides," Iseult said to the king. "We have only this man's word that the good minstrel has stolen his instrument. We must test this case, my lord."

"How?" the king asked.

Iseult evidently hadn't thought about that, but after a flustered moment, she said triumphantly, "By having both of the claimants play on the lyre to show who is best! It will be a trial by music."

"Very well," Tristram said. "I shall go first!"

The entire court burst into noise, as everyone except Dinadan and the queen eagerly assured Tristram that they had just heard his music and did not need to hear any more, thank you. King Mark ended the hubbub by standing, taking the lyre from Tristram's hands and walking across the court to hand it to Dinadan.

Dinadan blinked. Thomas had shown him once how to play the lyre, but at the time Dinadan had been too concerned with mastering his rebec to pay much attention. As revolting as Tristram's song had been, his skill with the lyre was clearly far beyond Dinadan's own. Then Dinadan looked about the throne room and saw the sympathetic, encouraging, even eager faces of the assembled courtiers and ladies. He smiled at Iseult. "Very well, but after I play, we must ask the decision from the entire court, not only of you and the king. Let the court decide."

"Hear, hear!" said several voices from the crowd.

Dinadan strummed the lyre once, then, improvising as quickly as he had ever done, sang,

> *"The finest singer isn't he*
> *Who has the greatest skill,*
> *But he who has the wit to see*
> *The time he should be still."*

Dinadan strummed the lyre once more, then bowed to the crowd, who hesitated, then applauded lustily.

"Hear, hear!"

"Beautiful! Beautiful!"

"Brought tears to my eyes!"

"He's the winner, all right!"

"Encore!... I mean *no* encore!"

"Hear, hear!"

It was unanimous. King Mark looked over the courtiers, then nodded to Dinadan to signify that the lyre was his. Dinadan bowed again, then turned and made his way back out of the throne room, followed by the grateful cheers of all assembled. He went directly to the stables, intending to leave at once, but he wasn't quick enough. As he led his horses out the stable door, Tristram ran up, his eyes wide and beseeching.

"Please, my friend, you must let me keep the lyre."

"No. It means much to me, as a gift."

"A gift from a peasant!"

"A gift from a man of skill and honour."

"But without it, I cannot woo my love! Surely you know that my heart belongs to her! Did you not hear the song of love I sang?"

"I heard it."

"And it had no effect on you?"

"Of course it did," Dinadan said, mounting his horse. "It made me feel dashed queasy." He booted his horse and trotted past Tristram, who stood alone and forlorn in the courtyard. Dinadan had one more obstacle to pass, though: at the front gate, clearly waiting for him, was Iseult. Dinadan reined in. "Good day, your highness."

Iseult didn't waste time. "You are the one who knew where the Lady Brangienne was."

Dinadan nodded slowly. "And you remember what I said – that if you harm her, I will sing stories of your infidelity across England."

Iseult nodded, and her eyes seemed to soften. "I know that. I no longer wish her harm. Please, I only want to tell her that she is safe from me now. I know that she would never feel comfortable serving me again, and so I do not offer her her old place, but I do wish to tell her that I was wrong and to ask her forgiveness."

Iseult's voice was heavy with emotion, and once she had to stop and wipe away tears. Watching her, Dinadan could see no sign that she was not sincere. Still, he was silent.

Iseult laid one hand on Dinadan's knee. "Could you not tell me where she is?"

Slowly, Dinadan shook his head. "No, your highness."

Iseult's eyes dropped. "I understand, and I do not blame you. But if you will not let me tell her myself, will you tell her for me?"

Dinadan took a deep breath. It was time to check on Brangienne anyway. "Very well, my lady." Then he rode through the gates and pointed his horses north, toward Brangienne's convent.

11

LOVE SONGS

Dinadan took his time on the way to Brangienne's convent. Though he missed Palomides, it was also pleasant to ride alone again. He played his rebec almost constantly, and everywhere he stopped, his playing drew an audience. In towns and alehouses, he attracted people. In the woods, he drew birds and small creatures. Sometimes when he was alone with the beasts he would put down the rebec and practise on Thomas's lyre, but judging from the way that the animals would then scatter, he needed a bit of work with his new instrument.

But by the end of the second day, Dinadan knew he was not really alone. Several times he had heard faint voices behind him, but although Dinadan rode slowly and stopped often, no one ever passed him. On the third day, Dinadan decided to wait for his reclusive followers. Coming to a thick copse where the trees grew so close together that they formed a nearly impenetrable screen, Dinadan hid his horses, then waited in the branches of a large elm tree. He didn't have to wait long. Not ten minutes had passed before two armed men in the livery of castle guards rode cautiously down the trail and then, as luck would have it, stopped just beneath him.

"Now where's the bugger gone?" the first guard muttered, half to himself.

"He must have rid on," the other replied. "He wouldn't have stopped in this thicket,"

"Wouldn't bet a groat on it, myself," the first guard said with a grunt. "Never saw such a fellow for stopping and picking daisies every bleedin' ten minutes. He wants to go somewhere, why doesn't he go there? That's all I want to know. We might have been done and back at the castle by now."

The other shrugged. "Don't mind the ride, myself. With Mark all in a rage, and the queen nasty to everyone, and now that new minstrel chap underfoot, I'd as soon be away from Tintagel anyway."

"Maybe, but the food's better there. We're getting low on rations already. If we don't find that sorceress and kill her soon, we'll have a hungry ride back to Cornwall."

"Come along then," the second guard said. "T'gaffer can't be too far ahead."

They rode on, and Dinadan let them go, seething with fury. So Iseult had sent these men to follow Dinadan to Brangienne and kill her – but why? What had she to gain by it? Dinadan waited another ten minutes, to give the guards ample time to get out of hearing, then he climbed down, retrieved his horses, and turned back toward Tintagel.

Dinadan was no closer to understanding Iseult's motives when he arrived at Tintagel, and the scene that met him there didn't help. The castle was in an uproar, with guards and knights scurrying about on urgent errands that had no visible purpose. Horses were being readied, hounds were baying, knights were giving each other contradictory commands, and at the centre of it all was a raging King Mark. It took Dinadan several minutes to find someone who would stop and explain, but at last he learned the cause of the commotion.

The minstrel "Tramtris" and Iseult had run away together the night before. Iseult had evidently concealed a knotted rope in her tower room, and had climbed down to meet Tramtris in the courtyard, and they had disappeared. It had been very well planned: Iseult had a key to the gate and had even fooled her chief lady-in-waiting into telling the king that Iseult was ill, with the result that their disappearance had gone unnoticed for almost a full day. King Mark had already had the lady-in-waiting executed and now was swearing revenge on whomever else he could blame.

Dinadan found a place in the shadows and watched while every guard and knight in the castle assembled before King Mark in the castle court. Mark drew himself up to his full height, which was not much, and gave his men their orders. These had to do with tearing Iseult and her lover to shreds and feeding them to the birds in tiny bits. Dinadan marvelled at the depth of the man's bitterness and hatred. When the king was done, the men galloped out the gates at top speed, charging headlong down the main road to the east, leaving King Mark alone in the yard. The king stood still for a moment, then sank to his knees and began to cry. Embarrassed, Dinadan looked away.

At length, the king went back inside the castle keep, and Dinadan rode away, his thoughts sombre. He had never asked to be involved in anyone else's love affairs, but he never seemed to be able to avoid them. It was enough to make a fellow swear off the whole ridiculous business of love. Either it was all a sham, as in the case of

Culloch and Olwen, or it was unbearably painful, as it seemed to be with King Mark, or it was selfish and cruel, as with Tristram and Iseult and Lamorak and his faery love. Dinadan would never understand why loving one person would make you want to hurt that person – or hurt someone else. It all left a sour taste in his mouth, and he longed to talk to someone sensible. It was past time to visit Brangienne.

He chose the least travelled path from Tintagel, taking a weedy track that meandered into a ridge of rocky hills, and within fifteen minutes, Dinadan knew that once again his evil muse had mired him in someone else's revolting love affair. Two sets of footprints marked the trail ahead of him, and one was definitely the print of a woman. Odd that Tristram and Iseult should have fled on foot. They couldn't possibly have expected to outrun the horses of their inevitable pursuers. They must have been going to a prearranged place, and not far away either. He knew he ought to turn right around and go the other way, but he didn't. He dismounted and followed their trail.

He found them twenty minutes later, in a small open area surrounded by craggy rock walls. Someone had expended a great deal of effort in preparing this rocky room for the lovers –

probably that lady-in-waiting that Iseult had left to be executed. There were ornate chairs and woven rugs scattered about, and golden candlesticks and dishes were stacked on tables. At one end of the area was the mouth of a cave, and over the cave's entrance was painted the legend "The Love Grotto". Tristram and Iseult lay together on a canopied bed, asleep in each other's arms. Revolted, Dinadan turned and crept back down the rocks to the trail, where he had left his horses. He thought once about returning to tell King Mark, but only for a second. For his part, he hoped he never saw any of them again. For the second time that week, he left Tristram and Iseult and rode away to Brangienne.

"I thought you'd come back," said the fierce-looking nun who had taken in Brangienne the last time Dinadan had been there. "I'm glad to see you." She smiled and didn't look fierce at all.

"And likewise, I'm sure," Dinadan managed to murmur politely.

The nun noted Dinadan's surprise and chuckled. "I'm afraid that I was not very civil to you when you brought Brangienne here. I do hope you'll forgive me."

"Oh, but, my lady —"

"Please do not call me that," the nun said calmly. "We have no titles here but sister – or, in my case, Mother. I am Mother Priscilla."

"Pleased to meet you... this time."

Mother Priscilla smiled again. "You should understand that you are not the first knight to bring a lady to our gates. Usually they do so when they have grown weary of the lady and are ready to discard her. I assumed that you were one of those, and by the time Brangienne had told me the truth, you were already gone. So I have been waiting these three months to apologise."

Now Dinadan understood. "Of course, my... ah... of course, Mother Priscilla."

"You'll be here to see Brangienne, I assume."

"Yes." Dinadan's brow creased. "But should you not say 'Sister Brangienne'?"

"No," Mother Priscilla said. "She has not taken her vows. But you are waiting, sir. I will bring Brangienne at once."

She walked quickly inside and reappeared a moment later with Brangienne. Brangienne's face lit with a brilliant smile when she saw Dinadan and she hurried forward, her hands outstretched. Dinadan took them in his own, returning her smile. "Dinadan!" she said. "How lovely to see you!" Her smile faded slightly. "You haven't come to take me away again, have you? Because, I warn you, I won't do it this time."

"No, no. I just thought I'd come check on you. You see, when I brought you here, Mother Priscilla seemed so formidable that I was afraid for your safety."

"Oh, that was because... oh, I see she's already explained that to you." Brangienne glanced once at Mother Priscilla.

"I have, dear. I'll leave you two alone now."

Brangienne's eyes laughed. "What? Alone with a man?"

"I hardly think you'll be in any danger here in the common yard. Goodbye, Brangienne."

Mother Priscilla strode away with a decisive step. "She's such a dear," Brangienne said, watching her depart. "She tries to be stern, but the sisters would do anything for her anyway, so it's hardly worth her bother."

"You're happy here, then?" Dinadan asked.

Brangienne nodded. "Yes. The only thing..." she hesitated.

"The only thing?"

"Sometimes I wonder if you're all right. But I can see you are. Tell me about things. What have you been up to since I've been here?"

Dinadan told her. It was odd that he who told

stories so often, to such varied audiences, should find it difficult to give a simple and unadorned account of his own life, but so it was. First he told her, very awkwardly indeed, how he and Palomides had gone to confront Iseult, and about the confusion caused by the magic horn and his final warning to Iseult. Brangienne coloured and looked at the ground, so Dinadan pressed on with his narrative. He told how he and Palomides had overcome Helius and Helake – leaving out the details of his fall into the river – and then told about Tristram's madness. Brangienne tried to look sympathetic at this, but not very successfully. Dinadan laughed, and said, "You don't care much, do you?"

"Not about Tristram," she replied promptly. "The difference between a madman and a nincompoop is not all that great, except that madmen probably do less harm. But don't let me interrupt you. Did he get better?"

Dinadan shook his head. "No. He just went back to being a nincompoop."

"How dull of him. But at least you're rid of him now. How did you manage that?"

"Actually, he did it himself. Along the way, I was given a lyre – a nice instrument, too – left to me by an old minstrel whom I had loved once. Anyway, Tristram saw it and —"

"He didn't steal it did he?" Dinadan nodded. Brangienne closed her eyes. "Tramtris again?"

Dinadan grinned affectionately at her. "You know, the thing I like most about you is your wit. I never have to bore myself by giving explanations."

"I suppose I should feel honoured, but since you've been riding with Tristram, it hardly counts. Your horses probably seem quick-witted in comparison."

"Yes, but I think you're even cleverer than my horses," Dinadan said with mock earnestness.

"Merci du compliment!" replied Brangienne, laughing. "Did you get your lyre back?"

Dinadan told her about the trial by music, and by the time he was done, she was wiping away tears of laughter. Dinadan let her get her breath, then said, more soberly, "Then something else happened. It's another reason I came back to see you. You see, once I'd gotten the lyre back, Iseult stopped me and said that she wanted to apologise to you, if I would tell her where you were."

"You didn't, did you?" Brangienne asked sharply.

"No, I'm not a fool twice. But I told her I'd give you the message."

"Were you followed?"

"Yes, by two guards with orders to kill you.

233

They lost my trail, though." He looked searchingly at Brangienne. "Why did she still want to kill you? It could do her no good."

Brangienne frowned. "You don't understand Iseult's kind of woman. She is always in competition with every other lady, and any woman that she ever sees as having an advantage over her – like knowing a secret – she will hate until one of them dies. She wants me dead because of something rotten inside her, not because it will serve any real purpose – which I'm sure it won't. I imagine that everyone in England knows about her affair with Tristram by now."

"If they don't, they soon will," Dinadan said. He told her how Tristram and Iseult had escaped and how he had found them in their "Love Grotto".

Brangienne sighed. "Idiots, of course. How long do they expect to be able to stay there undetected? How long will their food hold out? And how near did you say it was to Tintagel?"

"Not four miles."

"They're a tragedy waiting to happen. One of those pointless tragedies that are told by second-class minstrels."

Dinadan lifted one eyebrow and looked down his nose at Brangienne. "I wouldn't know," he said austerely.

Brangienne giggled, but said, "No, I'll give you this much. If there was ever a musician with God's own gift, it's you. Nothing second-class at all."

A moment later, Mother Priscilla joined them. "Brangienne, if you're coming in, it is time for you to join the others in the refectory."

Brangienne leaped to her feet. "If I'm coming in? But of course I'm – oh, goodness, is it already so late? I'm afraid I must have left others to do my chores before dinner!" She turned to Dinadan. "I have to go now, Dinadan. Thank you for coming. I've had so much fun talking with you. Are you satisfied that I'm all right now?"

Dinadan grinned and nodded. "Yes, but I'm almost sorry for it. It means I have no excuse to come visit you next time."

Mother Priscilla said calmly, "You need no excuse, Sir Dinadan. You may come as often as you like. But now it is time for you to go."

Dinadan had not been to Arthur's court in almost six months, and now that he had seen Brangienne, he began to long for Bedivere and Gaheris and his other friends there, so he pointed his horses toward Camelot. It was slow travelling, though, as he stopped at every likely tavern along the road to sing the new song he was working on – "The Ballad of Sir Palomides" – about how the noble Moorish knight had single-handedly defeated the two villainous brothers Helius and Helake. As a bit of history, it wasn't especially accurate, but Dinadan was pleased at how well he captured Palomides's honourable and generous nature, and surely a noble heart was something far more true than mere facts.

He was looking forward to sleeping in a bed in a quiet room when at last he came to Camelot, but it was not to be. The first person he saw upon riding through the castle gates was Bedivere, and the delight on his friend's face nearly brought a lump to Dinadan's throat. Then Bedivere spoke. "Dinadan! By all that's holy, it's wonderful to see you!"

"And likewise, Bedi —"

"You're just the person I've been wishing for!"

Dinadan's smile faded slightly. "For what, may I ask?"

"To go with me! I wanted you from the start, but you weren't here, and no one's heard from you in months. Kai wouldn't do it."

"Go where?" Dinadan asked warily.

"To Culloch's wedding, of course. The invitation came by special messenger just three days ago."

"Culloch's wedding! You don't mean —"

"That's right. Old Isbaddadon's finally given in."

"Or couldn't think of any more lame-brained chores for the silly sod to do. No, Bedivere, I'm with Kai this time. I want nothing to do with it."

Bedivere looked astonished. "But after all, Dinadan, you were with him at the start, even before I was. Don't you want to see how it all ends?"

"No."

Bedivere stared. "Well, haven't you ever felt even the least bit guilty about leaving the boy the way we did?"

"Not the least bit."

"Well, I have. Oh, I know it was the right thing to do, but I can't help thinking he might have been done years before this if we'd stayed with him. So you won't do it for Culloch?"

"No."

"How about for me? I don't want to go back there alone."

Dinadan looked at Bedivere for a long time. Finally he sighed. "The problem with being friends with a silly ass is that sometimes you end up doing silly things with him."

Bedivere smiled with sympathy. "Maybe it won't be so bad," he said hopefully.

Of course the wedding was as bad as anyone could

have imagined, and worse. It began with two weeks of nightly feasting, which to their immense gratification Bedivere and Dinadan missed. They arrived the day before the wedding, to be greeted by a gruff Isbaddadon and an excited Culloch. It didn't take long though to see that Culloch's excitement related not to the next day's wedding but to that evening's final feast. "Izzie is having all the men dress in black! Get it? As if it's a funeral instead of a wedding! Isn't that the funniest thing you've ever heard?" Then he laughed loudly and explained the joke to them all over again.

Bedivere and Dinadan chose not to attend these revels. As a result, they were the only two clear-eyed males present at the wedding the next morning. Being alert had its drawbacks, though. When it was time for the wedding to begin, and still no one had seen Culloch, it was Dinadan and Bedivere who ended up rousting the groom out of bed, splashing him down with cold water, dressing him in the best clothes they could find for him, then supporting him during the ceremony itself, which began all of two hours after it had been scheduled. By that time, at the altar, Lady Olwen was ready to spit fire, and even Isbaddadon, hardly in better shape than Culloch, was looking angry.

The priest intoned a long speech in words that

sounded vaguely like Latin but weren't ("Pure gibberish," Bedivere said later. "Fellow probably couldn't say more than two Latin words to save his life"), then switched to English to ask if Culloch took this lady to be his wife. Culloch answered with a faint snore. He had fallen asleep on his feet, leaning against Dinadan and Bedivere.

"You clodhead!" screamed Olwen. She drew back her left arm, made a very unladylike fist, and belted Culloch in the nose. "You drunken blot! You pig-faced, foul-smelling offal!"

Culloch rocked backwards, and Dinadan and Bedivere had to brace themselves to hold him up. King Isbaddadon clutched his head with both hands. "Yes, my love," he said, "but do you need to yell?"

"You, too!" Olwen shrieked. She tried to hit her father with the other fist, but that hand was holding a bouquet, and all she managed to do was shove a handful of flowers up the king's nose. With a squawk like a turkey pullet, Olwen threw down what was left of the bouquet and stomped away.

Everyone was silent for a moment. Then the priest looked timidly at the king. "Well then, I suppose it's off?"

Isbaddadon turned red. "Off? I should say not! My boy Culloch here has worked for three years and more for this! Am I Olwen's father or not? Am I king or not? On with the wedding!"

Dinadan and Bedivere glanced at each other in astonishment, and the priest gasped. "But, without the bride —"

"I'll answer for her!" the king declared. "Where were you? Oh, yes. 'Do you take this woman?' All right. She does!"

"Oh… ah… well then, Culloch, do you… um?"

Culloch hiccuped and started to sag, so Isbaddadon stepped in for him, too. "He does!"

"Well then, I – dear me, I've lost my place – oh, I pronounce you… er… man and wife."

The assembled guests gave a half-hearted cheer that died quickly. Dinadan glanced at Bedivere again, then shrugged and gave Culloch a push toward Isbaddadon. "Go ahead, lad. Kiss the bride. You coming, Bedivere?"

The two knights left Culloch in Isbaddadon's arms and strode firmly away. They didn't speak until they had saddled their horses and left Isbaddadon's castle behind them. Finally, Bedivere took a deep breath, let it out slowly, and said, "Sorry I talked you into coming, Dinadan. That was appalling. I've never seen the like."

"I was at a knighting ceremony a bit like that once," Dinadan replied. "Doesn't make it any less profane." After a moment he added, "On the bright side, the couple seems very well suited, don't you think?"

"Culloch and Isbad? Ay, they could have been made for each other."

"At any rate, they deserve each other." Dinadan made a face. "Love! The whole business is insane."

Bedivere glanced at Dinadan curiously. "Have you never met anyone you loved?"

"Don't think so. And it's something I'd remember, isn't it?"

"One would think," Bedivere said, his eyes still on Dinadan. "You know. I looked about the crowd at the wedding, but I never saw that lady we brought there that first day. What was her name?"

"Brangienne," Dinadan replied. "She's not there anymore." He grinned. "That may be the only good thing about that farce back there. It'll make a great story to tell Brangienne."

"Then you know where she is?"

"Oh, yes. She's well away from that madhouse, in a secret place."

Bedivere looked a question, but Dinadan avoided his eyes. He had already betrayed Brangienne's location by one careless comment, and he would not do it again. At length, Bedivere said, "You know, I had always thought that you and Brangienne were kindred souls."

Dinadan laughed. "We are, a bit, but how you could tell that from our first meeting is a wonder. You remember how we quarrelled. For years, I thought she hated me."

"But she doesn't?"

"Oh, no."

"And you? How do you feel about her?"

Slowly, Dinadan turned to look at Bedivere. "You mean... you thought... ? Oh no, Bedivere. There's been no talk of that sort of thing. No, really!"

"I see. Then she loves someone else?"

Dinadan almost laughed, remembering where Brangienne was. "No, I really don't think so," he replied.

Bedivere raised his eyebrows. "But you've not ever considered marrying her?"

"No, never."

"And has she ever considered marrying you?"

Dinadan blinked. "Now, how would I know that?"

Bedivere's voice was gentle. "By asking yourself if she has ever shown any interest in anyone but you. By asking yourself if perhaps the reason she has never married anyone else is because she loves you. By asking yourself how you would feel if she married someone else."

Dinadan's mind whirled, but he didn't speak.

"You say," Bedivere continued, "that Brangienne is in hiding. Why is that?"

"Oh," Dinadan replied, glad to have a question he could answer. "There is a powerful woman – never mind who it is – who won't rest until Brangienne's dead. The same one who sent those soldiers the time we first met her."

"Ah, so you're hoping this woman will come to think that Brangienne has already died?"

"No, not exactly. We just..." Dinadan trailed off. "But that's brilliant, Bedivere! All we have to do is convince her that Brangienne is dead, and she can have her life back! I don't know why I didn't think of that before! Thank you!"

Bedivere grinned. "I take it you're leaving me now?"

"Nothing personal, of course. It's just that now I know how to wrap this whole business up. You don't mind, do you?"

"Not at all. But Dinadan? Think about what I said, won't you?"

Dinadan nodded briefly – as if he could help thinking about it now that it had been spoken! – and wheeled his horse. He had to go one more time to Cornwall.

12

A SONG FOR A LADY

When Dinadan got to Cornwall, he made a wide circle around Tintagel and rode straight to the "Love Grotto", coming at it from the opposite direction. The hideaway was so well concealed that it took a few hours to locate it again, but at last he looked over the edge of the cliffs into Tristram and Iseult's retreat.

It was a mess. The furniture had been smashed, the carpets torn to bits, and all had been burned. The candlesticks and plates had been pounded into metal lumps and left to char in the fire. The painted words "Love Grotto" had been smashed off of the rock with a hammer. Brangienne had been right. They had not remained hidden for long.

Dinadan climbed down the rocks and examined

the room more closely. The fire was cold, and the ashes had been matted down by rain, from which Dinadan deduced that this had happened at least several days before. He found no bodies, though, or any other sign that the lovers had been destroyed along with their furnishings. He turned back to the wall to climb back to his horses and had taken his first step up when he heard a whisper of sound behind him. He started to turn, but he was too late. A powerful hand closed over his mouth, keeping him from making a noise. Strong arms pulled him back to the ground, and a sharp point pricked the skin just below his right ear.

"Who are you?" came a hoarse whisper. Dinadan tried to answer, but the hand over his mouth muffled his voice. "What? Speak up!" the whisper demanded.

It had to be Tristram. With an effort, Dinadan opened his mouth enough that he could nip the hand with his teeth. The hand jerked away for a second, and Dinadan said quickly, "I can't answer if you cover my mouth!"

"Oh." The arms relaxed and let Dinadan turn around, but the sharp point stayed at his throat. It was Tristram, all right, wielding a sharpened stick as a weapon. He wore about a week's worth of beard, and his eyes were as mad as they had ever been.

"It's me. Dinadan."

"Do I know you?" Tristram asked suspiciously.

"You never have," Dinadan replied. "But I know you all the same. What happened here? Was it Mark's soldiers? Where's Iseult?"

Tristram tensed and grasped his stick with both hands. "How do you know about Iseult and me? For I've spoken to no one. I've taken a vow of —"

Dinadan slapped away the sharp stick and snapped angrily at his brother. "Shut up! Do you hear me? Shut up, I say! Enough of this nonsense about a vow of silence. You flickerwick! Everyone in England knows that you and Iseult are having an affair, and do you know something? No one cares! The two of you are excessively boring, and no one is interested anymore except King Mark himself, and that's because he's as stupid as you are. Now put down that stick at once!"

Tristram let go of his stick, and for a moment his eyes seemed less glazed. "Dinadan?"

"Yes, Dinadan. Your brother."

"My brother?"

"Yes, you ass. Now answer my question. What happened here?"

Tristram sat down amid the rubble and began to sob. Dinadan sat, too, and let him cry for a while, then asked again. Finally, Tristram was able to tell him what he knew. Tristram had been out hunting – they had run out of food, as Brangienne had predicted – when King Mark's soldiers came and took Iseult. Tristram had heard the screams and had run to help, but by the time he arrived they were already galloping away on horses. The next day, King Mark had come back to the place himself, with all his soldiers, and they had methodically destroyed everything they could find. Tristram had watched them begin from a hiding place in the rocks, but had slipped away almost at once, hoping to rescue Iseult from Tintagel while the soldiers were busy.

"But it was no use," Tristram said. "Mark has her locked up in the highest tower room, and she is never permitted to leave it. I found a way to climb over the outer walls of the castle, but I couldn't climb the tower to her. Finally, she sent me away before Mark could return. I've been living in the woods ever since. Can you help me, Dinadan?"

Dinadan shook his head. "Not if you mean help you free Iseult. But I have some food with my horses. Come on, I'll give you something to eat."

They left the ruined grotto and climbed together back to the clearing where Dinadan's horses were. They made camp and ate together, and then Tristram rolled over and began sleeping fitfully. Dinadan watched him across the fire and wondered what to do. Once again, he was caught up in someone else's troubles. He had come intending to tell Iseult, with a great show of solicitude, that her beloved former lady-in-waiting Brangienne had died, so that Iseult would put her out of her mind, but now that hardly seemed worth doing. Iseult had problems of her own. Nevertheless, by trying to help one person, Dinadan had ended up embroiled in the ridiculous affairs of others. It was the story of his life.

He went to sleep that night still unsure about what to do next. He couldn't leave Tristram alone and mad in the forest and just ride away, but he could see no way to resolve Tristram's and Iseult's problems either. So it was with considerable relief that he awoke the next morning and discovered that Tristram had left him during the night. Dinadan smiled. There was nothing in his code of honour against allowing Tristram to leave him. Dinadan saddled his horses and gathered his gear, and then saw something that ruined his mood entirely. Thomas's lyre was missing.

Half an hour later, Dinadan rode up to the main gate of Tintagel Castle. Two guards with wicked-looking halberds – eight-foot long battleaxes with sharp points at the ends – stood there watching his approach. "Halt and state your business!" one said.

"He's all right," replied the other guard. "He's the minstrel fellow who took away the other chap's lyre. Remember?"

The first guard nodded, but he said, "We 'ave our orders, anyway. We're to send for the king as soon as anyone comes to the gate. You! Minstrel! You stay here while I fetch King Mark."

As soon as the first guard had left, Dinadan turned to the one who had recognized him. "It's been busy about here, hasn't it?"

"You've heard, then?"

"Yes. The minstrel Tramtris ran away with Queen Iseult, didn't he?"

"Huh! 'Tramtris' indeed. Sir Tristram is who it was, as everyone figured out when he took off with the queen. She's back, now."

"And what about Tristram?" Dinadan asked casually. "Have you seen him?"

The guard barked with laughter. "Not likely, is it? He'd have to be mad to show his face around here again."

"True," Dinadan said. "Very true."

King Mark must have been nearby, because at that moment he and the first guard appeared. "What do you want, sirrah?" Mark demanded.

Dinadan decided to be blunt and honest. "Same

thing as last time," he said. "Tristram stole my lyre again, and I've come to get it back."

"Well, he's not here," Mark said.

"He will be," Dinadan replied. "And he doesn't need the gate. He's found a way over the wall."

Mark laughed and repeated what the guard had just said. "He'd have to be mad."

"He is," Dinadan said calmly. "May I come in and wait for him?"

"No!" Mark snapped. "No one comes in! Maybe you're after my wife, too? Eh? What do you say to that?"

Dinadan looked into Mark's eyes and saw in them as much madness as he had ever seen in Tristram's. "I couldn't begin to say —" he began. But he got no further. From across the courtyard, from the base of the tallest tower of the castle, came the unmistakable sound of a lyre.

Mark's eyes widened, and he made a strangled sound in his throat as they all looked across the yard. There was Tristram, his back to the gate, blithely strumming on Thomas the Rhymer's lyre. Mark growled, like a wounded dog, and grabbed one of the guards' halberds.

"No!" Dinadan shouted. He reached out to grab Mark, but the closed gate was between them. Mark pointed the halberd at Tristram's back and began running. Dinadan shouted urgently, "Stop, Mark! Tristram! Turn around!"

At the topmost window of the tower, Iseult appeared. She saw Tristram, then saw Mark charging him. She screamed and leaned out the window. "Stop! No! My love!"

The halberd took Tristram square in the centre of the back. He made no noise, but simply sprawled forward, apparently dead before he hit the paving stones. Iseult screamed again and clutched at the air, and then her scream of grief changed to one of fear as she overbalanced and fell. She landed with a thump at King Mark's feet, and then all was quiet. Mark stared at Tristram's body, then at Iseult's, and then he fell forward in a faint.

Dinadan and the guards stared, unmoving, at the little heap of bodies across the court. At last the friendly guard said, "Would you like me to fetch your lyre for you, sir?"

Dinadan shook his head. "Bury it with Tristram," he said. Then he turned and rode away.

Mother Priscilla greeted Dinadan with a warm smile. "I knew you would return," she said, "but I did not think it would be so soon."

"I didn't plan to be back so soon myself," Dinadan replied. "But I've something to tell

Brangienne that's rather important,"

Mother Priscilla nodded. "I will send for her at once. Come out to the garden. Would you care for a glass of our own blackberry wine while you wait?"

Dinadan accepted the wine and went to the convent garden, where he sat on a rough wooden bench. A minute later, Brangienne appeared, her cheeks flushed with pleasure. "Dinadan! What brings you back so soon?"

"Several things," he replied. "It's been a busy fortnight since I was here last."

"Why? What's happened?"

Dinadan licked his lips and hesitated. "Why don't you go first? Tell me about your life here. Last time all we did was talk about my affairs."

Brangienne looked acutely at Dinadan's face, but she said, "Very well," and began to tell Dinadan about life at the convent. She described the very ordinary routine, the hours of solitude, the hours of working alongside all her friends there, and the sense of peace that had grown inside her. "Perhaps you had not noticed," she said, "but I was not always very peaceful before I came here."

"Really?" Dinadan said politely.

"I was angry at everyone, I think. Knights, ladies, kings, lovers, men, women – have I left anyone out?"

"No, that should cover it. But you aren't angry now?"

Brangienne's lips quivered. "Not... not usually. There are a few of the sisters who are, shall we say, irritants. They are good hearted enough, just not extremely clever, and sometimes I do need to say an extra prayer for patience. But no, I don't live with anger anymore."

"That's good," Dinadan said, for lack of anything else to say.

"Now, suppose we get on with what you came here for. What has happened that sent you back her to see me so soon?"

Still Dinadan was loath to begin. "After I left you, I went to a wedding," he said. Brangienne lifted her eyebrows in question, and Dinadan grinned. "Culloch and Olwen."

Brangienne rolled her eyes. "Oh. Well, I suppose I wish them very happy."

"Can't imagine either of them being happy," said Dinadan reflectively. "Whether they're married or not. But they're not off to the best start." He proceeded to tell her about the wedding, and when he was done, she could only shake her head, aghast.

"What fools some people choose to be," she

said. Then she looked again at Dinadan. "But surely that isn't what you came to tell me."

"No." There was nothing left but to say it. "Iseult is dead."

"Dead," Brangienne repeated slowly. "How? By violence?"

"I suppose you could say that." Dinadan told her the story, simply and plainly and without emotion.

Brangienne looked at the ground. "I loved her once, when we were children. I suppose I was never more than a servant to her, but I thought we were more. What a dreadful, horrible, stupid, meaningless death to die."

"But of course it won't be long before the minstrels are telling it as if it were noble somehow, making it a great tragic love story."

"You won't, will you? No, of course you won't."

Dinadan shook his head. "I thought you ought to know, though, that the person who wanted you dead is gone. You're safe now."

Brangienne nodded to herself, her eyes empty, and Dinadan could see she was lost in thought. He was silent for several minutes, waiting for her. His stomach began to tighten, and his mouth grew dry. It became harder and harder to breathe normally. At last Brangienne looked up. "Thank you for coming to tell me, Dinadan."

Dinadan nodded. "Brangienne?"

"Yes?"

"I have something else to ask you, too."

"What?" her voice was very quiet.

Dinadan took the hurdle at a rush. "Would you like to marry me?"

Brangienne was silent for a long time. "Dinadan, you are the only man on earth that I could ever marry," she said at last. Dinadan swallowed, and the tight feeling in his chest seemed about to burst. "But if you don't mind terribly, I think I'd rather not."

Dinadan let his breath out with deep sigh. "Oh, thank God," he said.

Brangienne burst into merry laughter. "What do you mean?" she said at last. "Don't you *want* to marry me?"

Dinadan was laughing, too. "I feel just as you do, my love. I could never marry anyone else, but no, no, I don't want to marry you."

"Then why did you ask, you idiot? Suppose I had said yes?"

"It was something that Bedivere said after Culloch's wedding. He said he's always thought there was something between us."

"Well, there is, isn't there?"

"Of course there is, though dashed if I know what to call it. But he put the idea in my head that you were in love with me and would never marry anyone else because you were waiting for me to ask."

"Oh," Brangienne said. "I understand. So you screwed up your courage and asked me because you were afraid it was the only thing that would make me happy."

Dinadan shrugged. "Something like that."

Brangienne leaned forward and kissed Dinadan lightly on the forehead. "You're such a dear, my love."

A voice from behind them said, "Then it's all settled?" It was Mother Priscilla.

"What do mean, Mother?" Brangienne asked.

She looked at Dinadan. "Did you ask her to marry you?"

Brangienne's eyes widened. "You knew he would?"

"Of course, you silly girl. Why do you suppose I've never let you take your vows? You had to face this first. So?"

Dinadan stood from the bench and bowed to Mother Priscilla. "Yes, I asked her. And she's made me the happiest man on earth."

"Ah, she has, has she?" Mother Priscilla

said quietly.

Brangienne giggled. "Yes, I have. I turned him down."

Dinadan sat cross-legged on his saddle and played his rebec. He was riding more or less in the direction of Camelot, but if he missed it, he didn't care much. Other knights of King Arthur's court were always riding out on quests – very intent on going to particular places to perform particular tasks – but Dinadan had come to accept that he was not like that. For him, it was enough to go, without necessarily arriving anywhere. Every time he had gone somewhere specific it had been with someone else or against his wishes for someone else's sake. "I suppose that means that I'll never accomplish as much as those other fellows," he said aloud. "Thank heaven for that, anyway."

He played idly on his instrument for a moment, then began to sing, quietly, a little nonsense ditty he had been fooling about with since leaving Brangienne the day before,

> *"When I was but a little tiny boy,*
> *With a hey, ho, the wind and the rain,*
> *A foolish love was but a toy,*
> *For the rain, it raineth every day.*

"But when I came to man's estate,
  With a hey, ho, the wind and the rain,
  Love's foolishness I came to hate,
  For the rain, it raineth every day.

"At last I learnt to be a friend,
  With a hey, ho, the wind and the rain,
  And found a love that doesn't end,
  Though the rain, it raineth every day.

"A great while ago, the world begun,
  With a hey, ho, the wind and the rain,
  But that's all one, my song is done,
  And I'll strive to please you every day,
  To please you every day."

AUTHOR'S NOTE: THE SINGERS OF TALES

All the stories I tell about King Arthur and his knights have been told before, some of them hundreds of times. The story of Culloch and the tasks he must do for the hand of the fair Olwen, for instance, is an ancient Welsh story, "How Culhwch Won Olwen," which is found in a collection of Welsh tales called *The Mabinogion*. All the tasks that I show Culloch doing are from that original story – including such inane tasks as weaving a leash from the beard of Dillus the Bearded. Whoever he was.

The most important source for my book, though, is the story of Tristram (or Tristan) and Iseult (or Isoud or Isolde or Isolt). The story has been told for centuries, and there are ancient versions in French, German, Italian, English, and even Norwegian. I've used two of these ancient accounts, the wonderful version by the German poet Gottfried von Strassburg and the much more long-winded retelling by Sir Thomas Malory in his *Morte d'Arthur*. From these two accounts I took the basic love potion mix-up plot, along with such details as the Horn of Infidelity and the Love Grotto. I also appropriated several minor characters, such as Brangienne (sometimes called Bragwaine) and Sir Lamorak and Sir Palomides.

In Malory's version appears the knight named Dinadan, who for some reason often finds himself with Tristram, though he doesn't seem to like Tristram very much. Dinadan's a very minor, but memorable, character in Malory, and as I read the story of that thoroughly depressing pair of lovers, Tristram and Iseult, I found myself liking Dinadan more and more by comparison. He jokes and sings and tells tales and – most rare for a Malory knight – occasionally turns down a fight. Here, I thought, was a knight who deserves his own story, and so I've used Dinadan as a new way to tell this tale that has been told so many times before.

Or sung, I should add. You see, the oldest of the Arthurian stories were not originally written down, or even told. They were set to music and sung by professional singers – called minstrels or troubadours in England, *trouvères* or *jongleurs* in France, and *minnesingers* in Germany. Many of these artists could neither read nor write but could recite heroic tales in perfect poetic rhythm from memory for hours at a time. Or, if they didn't have hours, they might sing ballads, love songs, or little poetic riddles. The songs that I have Dinadan and Wadsworth the minstrel sing are almost all based on real songs from the Middle Ages or Renaissance. There really is a song called "My Lief is Faren in Londe" (although the original's better than the one I present) and there really is a line in a Renaissance poem that goes "Cuckoo, jug-jug, pu-we, to-witta-woo."

Okay, so it wasn't the crowning moment of English literature. They weren't all Shakespeare. But without these minstrels, even Shakespeare wouldn't have been Shakespeare. What I mean by that is that even the greatest poets of the Renaissance Shakespeare and Dante – owed much to the minstrels. Both of them knew the old songs well and used them often in their own works. (In fact, the ditty that Dinadan sings at the end of the last chapter is borrowed and adapted from the end of Shakespeare's *Twelfth Night*.) Since everyone who writes in English owes a debt to Shakespeare, then we also owe much to these anonymous poets, these early performance artists, these marvellous singers of tales.

Gerald Morris

THE SQUIRE'S TALES

BOOK I

SQUIRE TERENCE AND THE MAIDEN'S KNIGHT

GERALD MORRIS

When Terence, a young orphan, meets an aspiring
knight named Gawain, he embarks on the adventure of a
lifetime. Gawain is headed for King Arthur's Camelot
and asks Terence to join him as his squire. On their
quest, they encounter a thrilling world of sorcery, spells
and sword fights. Their journey takes them to a
magical realm, where Terence discovers the secret of his
past and undertakes a challenge only he can face.

ISBN 0 7534 1350 7

THE SQUIRE'S TALES

BOOK II

SIR GAWAIN, HIS SQUIRE AND HIS Lady

GERALD MORRIS

Squire Terence and Sir Gawain are off questing again, but this time they have a grim destination. Gawain is set to meet the Green Knight in a contest that will surely end in his death. Along the way, the knight and his squire have a slew of hair-raising adventures and meet a feisty damsel-in-distress named Eileen. As they weave their way between the world of men and the faery world, Terence finds love and Gawain confronts the true nature of honour and courage.

ISBN 0 7534 1351 5

THE
SAVAGE DAMSEL
AND THE DWARF

GERALD MORRIS

Her family's castle besieged by an evil knight, Lady
Lynet sets out for King Arthur's court, accompanied by a
strange dwarf, Roger, to recruit a rescuer. But the only
person who volunteers to help is a scruffy serving boy,
Beaumains. The three travel to Lynet's castle,
encountering danger, magic and many unusual characters,
including the famous knight Gawain and his squire,
Terence. Through their amazing adventures, Lynet
discovers that people can be far more than they seem, and
surprises even herself.

ISBN 0 7534 1352 3

THE SQUIRE'S TALES

BOOK IV

PARSIFAL'S PAGE

GERALD MORRIS

Piers is desperate to become a knight's page and escape the dirt and noise of his father's blacksmith shop. But Parsifal, the aspiring knight that he serves, is not the sort of master he had in mind. Although brave and strong, Parsifal is unschooled in courtly behaviour. On their adventure-filled travels, Piers slowly begins to realize that being a knight has nothing to do with shining armour and tournament victories. As they quest for the elusive Holy Grail, Piers and Parsifal learn about the true nature of knighthood – and about themselves.

ISBN 0 7534 1353 1